The Wolf's Bane Saga

Book Five

I0647766

Moon Rise

M. KATHERINE CLARK

Other Works by M. Katherine Clark

The Greene and Shields Files:
    Blood is Thicker Than Water
    Once Upon a Midnight Dreary
    Old Sins Cast Long Shadows
    Tales from the Heart, Novelettes
Soundless Silence a Sherlock Holmes Novel
The Rest is Silence, an Edmond Holmes Novel – Coming Soon
Love Among the Shamrocks Collection:
    Under the Irish Sky
    Across the Irish Sea
    On the River Shannon
    The Land Across the Sea, an Emmet O'Quinn Short
Love Among the Shamrocks Collection, The Next Generation:
    In Dublin Fair City
    Song of Heart's Desire
    Chasing After Moonbeams – Coming Soon
The Wolf's Bane Saga:
    Wolf's Bane
    Lonely Moon
    Midnight Sky
    Star Crossed
    Moon Rise
    Moon Song, a Companion
Silent Whispers, a Scottish Ghost Story
Dragon Fire
    Heart of Fire
    Will of Fire – Coming Soon

The final installment, this is dedicated to all those who helped get to this point! Lucky number thirteen! Let's celebrate the Saga together! Slainte!

Prologue

"Giorsal!" Caylean bellowed, jerking awake. Blinking and looking around the clearing, seeing the trees and the Irish Sea across the way, Caylean's chest constricted. He had left his home just the other day but, unlike Dagda, he was unable or unwilling to travel with the speed of the gods.

Knowing the moment Giorsal's heart broke, he gulped in large deep breaths. She had read his note and it nearly destroyed her. Their connection still so strong, his chest felt as if someone or something was squeezing his heart so tightly. Letting out a short cry, he wrapped his arms around his knees and buried his face.

"Oh gods, Giorsal," he sobbed. "Forgive me, my love.

Please. Understand why I did what I did. I never wanted to leave you—"

"Then why did you?" He heard Dagda's voice. Not seeing his mentor, Caylean felt the words and heard them in his mind.

"Dagda, are you with her?" he questioned.

"Nay, we are coming after you," he revealed.

"Who?"

"At least one person who wants your head."

"Oh gods," he sobbed. "Tristan?"

"Aye, we found Giorsal," Dagda shared the memory of seeing her curled on the floor sobbing. Caylean let out a tortured moan.

"Gods, nay," he wailed. "I am sorry. Dagda, you must help her understand why. Please, ease her broken heart. I beg you. You told me I am like a son to you, I beg you, if that is true, ease her."

"Easy, lad," Dagda replied. "Her aunts are helping, and I gave Isla a spell to help her. But my concern is you. Why did you leave?"

"I had to," he argued. "I cannae control myself!"

"You did not need to leave her," he scolded. "You could have come to me or waited for me. I was on my way. We can figure this out. Have you forgotten my cousin was a hybrid? I would have helped you. Giorsal needs you now more than ever."

"What? Why?" Caylean snapped. Dagda went quiet and no matter how hard Caylean tried, he could not break the silence nor read his mind. "Tell me, Dagda is she ill? What happened?"

"I will not be the one to tell you," he stated. "But you should have spoken to her and waited for me. Now, enough of this running and tell me where you are." Caylean's mind went blank. "Tell me, lad or I swear to you, Tristan will not be the only one who is angry with you."

"You may hate me all you desire, Dagda. Nothing compares to how much I hate myself."

"I do not hate you, lad," Dagda replied. "I am saddened you did not come to me."

"How could I?" he asked.

"Easily," Dagda stated. "I have always told you to come to me."

"I am a danger to everyone around me. I killed my own people!"

"Aye, and we can learn how to control it."

"How?"

Dagda was quiet for a moment. "Do you want to give it up? Power can be a difficult thing to release once you have tasted it."

"I would, but I donnae ken how and I will nae put my mate in danger," Caylean said.

"You released her, she is no longer your mate," Dagda replied.

The pain of his words struck Caylean deep in his heart. "I could have killed her," he stated.

"Aye, but you did not," Dagda replied. "You should come back."

"You are asking me to put her in danger," he said.

"I am asking you, is this what you truly want? Do you want to live with the knowledge of Giorsal being free to mate with someone else? Do you want to see her happy with another male?" Visions of Geileis' intertwined with Flynn flashed in Dagda's mind but the woman's face changed to Giorsal and Caylean growled.

"Stop! That is you, that is nae me," Caylean replied. "Giorsal would nae do that."

"You have no claim on her," Dagda shouted. Then after a

moment, he took a deep breath and calmed. "I am sorry to shout but you have no idea the pain one feels. I will not allow you to feel the same. You are Giorsal's mate."

Caylean was quiet and something inside him snapped.

"No' anymore," he said and with strength he had never felt before, Caylean broke the link between them.

Chapter One

"Dammit," Dagda cursed as he fell back.

"What?" Tristan demanded.

"He shut me out," Dagda stood and looked at the three men traveling with him. "I was able to speak with him. He *was* on his way to my grove but now... I am not sure where he is going."

"What do you mean?" Tristan demanded.

"He hates himself for what he's done, but he hates what he *is* more," Dagda said.

"Maybe if you could get to him again, I could speak with him," Aedan offered.

"He will not let me back in," Dagda replied. "I do not think you understand how strong your son is. In some respects, he is stronger than me."

"Then what good are you?" Tristan demanded.

Dagda raised a hand in peace, "I am not the enemy here, Tristan."

"Aye? Well, you seem to conveniently allow him to slip away."

"Are you saying my son is an enemy, Tristan?" Aedan asked.

"Aye, he is," Tristan replied. "He left my daughter hurting, alone, and carrying his pup."

"I still do not understand how that happened," Dagda muttered.

"If you need an explanation on *how* that happened, you have no' lived the life my grandson has told me you have," Weylyn said.

"I know how," Dagda answered. "What I do not know is *how.* Caylean is a druid. He has the protective spell cast over him to prevent him from fathering children just as your mates have to prevent them from conceiving. He should not have been able to impregnate Giorsal."

"Unless he removed the spell," Aedan offered. "Isla has in the past."

"Knowing Caylean's history with the act of lovemaking, I doubt very much he did," Dagda explained.

"What do you mean? His history?" Weylyn asked. "He has told you about he and Giorsal?"

"Nay, I meant when he was in my grove," Dagda said.

"Uh, Dagda," Aedan stopped him. "I think what you meant to say is, Caylean has told you about Giorsal... aye?" he prompted.

Dagda looked at him and raised a brow, but then scoffed. "You wolves, so adamant there is no other way to mate than with your true one. It may shock your maidenly sensibilities to know, in my grove, we bed any female the gods decree. Caylean has known the pleasures of the flesh, I was there when he first learned."

"What?" Tristan roared. "How dare he. And you," he turned to Aedan. "You knew? And yet you still allowed him to mate my daughter?"

"I did nae *allow* my son or your daughter to do anything, Tristan," Aedan rebuttaled. "They are grown. They make their own decisions. I donnae believe Caylean would have kept that from her and if she knew and mated him anyway, then I believe she truly loves him."

"Though it is uncommon, it is no' unheard of," Weylyn started. "Now, I would like to stop speaking of my grandson's intimate life and move on to where he was when Dagda spoke with him."

"We are no' done speaking of this," Tristan stated.

"We are done," Dagda replied. "You are not to force your ideas upon to another. That is not what being Alpha is, Tristan. You are merely to keep them safe and guide them."

"Who do you think you are? Giving directions as if you own us?" Tristan demanded.

"Tristan donnae do this," Weylyn pleaded.

"You are no' alpha. You donnae tell me what to do," Tristan went on as if his mentor had not spoken.

"You are right, I am not your Alpha, but I am an Alpha," Dagda replied.

"That does nae give you the right to tell me what to do"

"Aye, it does. We are no longer on your land. This is my land, my home. My people. When the Romans invaded your precious Britannia in 55 B.C, the people of this land roamed wild and free. Once the legionnaires pushed back the wild and untamed Celts, they built a wall; Antoine's Wall, it was once magnificent, once imposing... trust me, I was there, I saw it. But it was not the humans they feared, but us, *my* people. I am the son of the first family. You *will* listen to me or you can find him on your own. Do you understand me?" The command in Dagda's voice overpowered the other two, but Tristan let out a roar and charged him.

With a twist of his wrist, the dark druid froze Tristan in place and looked over at Weylyn and Aedan; poised to defend their alpha.

"Will I need to freeze you too?" Dagda questioned.

"Release our alpha, Druid," Weylyn said calmly. "We agree we need you to find Caylean, but we will defend our alpha if needed."

"I respect that, Weylyn and I respect your peaceful words, however I cannot expose my people to his anger."

"Then calm him as you did Caylean at Gregor's wedding," Aedan offered.

"I have. The entire journey so far. But he is stronger than most, being Alpha. I will not allow a male like Marrock loose on my land," Dagda explained.

"He is nothing like Marrock. I give you my word," Weylyn promised. "He is angry due to his daughter's pain. You are nae a father, I donnae believe. Are you?"

"Caylean is as close to me as a son."

"But you have nae blood pups," Weylyn stressed.

"Nay, I do not," he answered.

"Then you cannae possibly understand the pain he is feeling. Our pups are connected to us in the most primal way possible," Weylyn placed a hand on Aedan's shoulder. "Their pain is ours as surely as they feel it. Pardon his rashness. Though he is grown, and his heart is that of an alpha, he is channeling his daughter's pain as if it was his own. I doubt his reunion with Caylean will be without a fight."

"I will stop him if it is. He can fight me no' my son," Aedan said.

"I donnae believe that will be best, lad," Weylyn stated. "His fight is with Caylean and though I love that lad, he is to blame for Giorsal's plight. You cannae take Tristan's right to avenge his daughter's grief."

"Though I donnae agree with Caylean's choice to leave, I do understand it," Aedan said. "He did nae want to harm his lass or anyone else in his family."

"If you had told me about him attacking you sooner, Aedan I would have been better equipped to handle him earlier," Dagda stated.

"I said nothing about him attacking me," Aedan turned to the dark druid.

"Aye, so I read your mind," Dagda replied.

"You have nae right to do so."

"Nay, but it is my right to know all that affects my people and make no mistake Caylean is part of my people, even though he is your son. Now, I will release your alpha but if he attacks me, I have every right to defend myself as we are no longer on his land."

Weylyn stepped between his alpha and Dagda, facing Tristan. "Can he hear us?"

"He can," Dagda confirmed.

Weylyn nodded and took one more step closer to him. "Lad, you must control yourself. 'Tis my honor to be led by you, but this is no' you. I ken the pain you feel, the anger, but, my lad, stay your claws for now until we ken Giorsal is safe. I beg of you. Donnae make a liar out of me. You are no' your father. I could never love you as much as I do if you were."

He saw Tristan's eyes soften and turned to Dagda.

Nodding to him, Weylyn caught Tristan as he fell forward when Dagda released him. Tristan trembled in his arms but said nothing.

"Aedan, Dagda could you give us a moment?" Weylyn asked. Aedan and Dagda nodded and left the two alone for a moment. Tristan stood on his own and stepped away from Weylyn, turning his back to his Beta.

"'Tis all right to let out your pain, lad. I have never thought less of you when you have in the past," Weylyn said.

"I am alpha now, no' some pup," Tristan replied heatedly.

"You will always be my alpha, but you also will always be the son I did nae have when I raised you. Donnae keep your pain bottled up. That is what happened to your father," Weylyn cautioned.

"I am no' my father," Tristan was adamant as he turned back to face him.

"Aye, I ken, lad. You donnae need to convince me. But now I ask you to let your pain go," Weylyn said.

"I cannae. 'Tis all I have right now."

"Nay," Weylyn's harsh tone shocked him. "'Tis no', you have love. The love of your mate, the love of your pups and the love of your pack. You cannae let your anger for Caylean consume you. 'Tis no' worth it. All it takes is one time, then the next time and the next until you are like him. I will never allow it. You are of my blood, too. You are of your mother's blood. Donnae think for a moment I will let you become your father."

"You will no' *let* me? You forget yourself, Weylyn," Tristan spat.

"I donnae. I ken well my station in your pack for it was my father's station in your grandfather's and Marrock's. I donnae challenge you in any way, apart from challenging you to see the truth. Let go of your anger."

"You donnae have a right to challenge me for anything, Dog," Tristan bellowed.

For one horrifying moment, Weylyn saw Marrock's shadow cross Tristan's face then the regret of his words broke Tristan. His eyes grew large and he gasped. "Oh, dear gods, Weylyn, I am so sorry."

Weylyn ignored the prickling on the back of his neck. Tristan rushed to his dearest friend but pulled back when Weylyn took one step back, the hair on Weylyn's arms rising. Horrified at what he said and Weylyn's reaction to him, Tristan fell to his knees.

"I am so sorry, my friend. I am angry at the lad. He hurt my little lass and I want revenge. I am so sorry to have taken it out on you. Please forgive me."

"I do, lad but this shows me your father's hold on you is stronger than I hoped," Weylyn offered his hand to Tristan.

Standing, Tristan looked down, unable to meet his mentor's eyes.

"I have felt his presence strongly since Eion's betrayal. I fought it, but Dagda's challenge and Caylean's betrayal pushed me over the edge. I am horrified at my response. I will apologize to Dagda and Aedan. I ask you to keep me in check, my friend. I donnae wish to be anything like my father."

"Be like him in one regard," Weylyn stepped forward. "His passion. When Marrock put his mind to it, he fought for it with everything inside him. Some.... most of the time, it was the wrong thing, but his passion was unbreakable."

"I defer to your knowledge on my father, Weylyn," Tristan stated. "As you ken, we were nae close."

"Nay, I ken, lad. But now let us get on with our journey. I would still like to be young when this is over." Weylyn's tease broke the mood and Tristan chuckled but there was still caution in Weylyn's eyes.

"Time is something we have plenty of, my friend. Come

now, let us continue. I thank you for your counsel, but I fear my anger may resurface when I see the lad."

"You have my permission, as his grandfather to strike him once, for his father and I intend to do the same. But nae more."

"I thank you for your permission. Though I donnae need it."

"I ken. But I will stop you if you do more than once. And if you recall, though I cannae beat you in sparing, I will put up a fight."

"As I donnae intend to fight you, Weylyn, I will say, if the lad is reasonable, I will suppress my urge to tear his throat out. But if he is nae..."

"That is something we will cross when we see him again."

"Tell me something, what did Dagda mean just now when he spoke to Aedan? What attack was he referring to?"

"That is something Aedan will need to tell you," Weylyn called the other two over and Tristan apologized to them both. Once they accepted his apology, he turned to Aedan and asked his burning question.

Aedan looked over at his father. "Donnae look at him, he did nae tell me, but I need to ken. Tell me."

Aedan huffed and relayed what happened when he and Weylyn went in search of Caylean after he was struck with the wolf's bane arrow. Tristan took a step forward, concern ripping through him. His eyes went to Aedan's shoulder where no visible marks marred his skin.

"The blood, that was yours?"

"Aye."

"But nae marks?"

"Caylean has the power to heal without scar," Dagda explained.

"Are you all right?" he breathed.

"Thanks to Caylean," he said.

"That lad is troubled," Tristan shook his head. "He does one thing that is good and another that is evil."

"He has done no evil, Tristan," Dagda spoke up. "Believe me. He dabbled in darkness with me," Dagda motioned to his markings but continued. "But he has done little in the ways of evil."

"That is no' what I meant. But he causes pain."

"I know it is difficult for you, Tristan. You do not want your daughter hurt, and had I been blessed with children, I would feel the same, but as much as I care for all, Caylean has become like a son to me. I know he did wrong by your daughter, but he is a good male. Right now, he needs your love and support not your scorn. I know you would like to kill him for how he treated Giorsal, but in his mind, he wanted to protect her. He believes whatever he is, in uncontrollable."

"Can he be controlled?" Aedan asked.

"We will stop and speak with my father, he will know," Dagda stated.

"Your father?" Weylyn asked. "Who is he?"

"One who will know what to do."

"You have been vague about your family since I met you," Tristan said. "And you said earlier you were the son of the first family. What does that mean?"

"All will be revealed," he replied cryptically. "But now, come, my friends. A storm approaches. I feel it. We must make it across the sea to Erin before it comes."

They walked on, but Aedan hung back with his father. "He speaks in riddles," he whispered.

"Aye," Weylyn answered. "I have my suspicions about him but nothing definite."

13

"You ken who he is?" Aedan asked.

"There was a legend," Weylyn said. "But I donnae ken how true it is."

"Tell me tonight," Aedan offered. "I will take first watch, perhaps you could tell me then."

"Aye, I will."

"We cross here," Dagda called back.

During the day, they were phased as wolves, running at wolf speed to catch up with Caylean. Dagda, the largest of all of them and the darkest. He was a black wolf and his markings were still visible when he was phased. The marking across his eye decorated his fur. Reaching the port of Scotland to Skye and then beyond to Erin was easily done. But not seeing a boat to carrying them over, Aedan looked around and spoke.

"Are we to swim?" he asked. "Or will you transport us a different way?"

Dagda said nothing, but when he turned from them, he walked into knee deep water, half-phased, and howled. An answering shout in the distance, covered by the fog, echoed to the shore. Soon, a boat was visible with two men navigating. Dagda waded deeper into the water and pulled the schooner further to shore. One man greeted Dagda with a warrior's shake.

"If we cross now, we will be ahead of the storm," the man said.

"Have you seen another? Caylean journeys this way," Dagda replied.

"Not this way, my lord," the other male still on board the boat, answered. "We have been here all day."

"Then he must have made the crossing further down," Dagda turned to the others and nodded. "Come aboard."

"Who are they?" Tristan asked.

"We have no time," Dagda replied. "I know them, and trust them, now come aboard."

"Not until you tell us who they are," Aedan said, stepping in front of Tristan and Weylyn. "I will no' have my alpha and my father get in that boat until I am satisfied they are nae a threat."

"They are not a threat," Dagda stated.

"'Tis all right, Dagda," one of the men said. "We waste time arguing and as good of swimmers as we are, we will no' be able to navigate these waters for you once the storm hits." Turning to Aedan, the older male continued. "I assume since you are the most vociferous of your alpha's safety as well as the weapons you carry, you are the war chief of your clan."

"Aye," he answered. "I am."

"Then, I will show you what we are," he said. "And if it is acceptable, please get into the boat quickly so we donnae lose you all in the storm."

"I agree," Aedan said.

The man nodded to the younger one and he hopped out of the boat, passing Dagda who grabbed his arm. "No, Glinyeu, Sion you do not have to do this."

"We waste too much time arguing," the older one said. "Let him be, Dagda. We believe these are good people. We would no' come to you if we did nae trust you."

The younger man looked up at the older one, still on the boat. "Go ahead, son. I ask you no' to make any sudden noises or movements. He will nae harm you."

Dagda let go of the young man's arm and he took a deep breath. Lowering into the water, he disappeared beneath the waves. When he resurfaced the black eyes of a seal looked back at them. Though he still looked somewhat human, he lifted his tail showing a fin of a mermaid. The boy disappeared under the water again and when he rose, he was human once more.

"Does that answer your question?" Dagda demanded.

"You are mermen?" Weylyn questioned.

"Selkies," the male corrected.

"I thought they were myths," Weylyn said.

"As we thought most wolves were too," he answered helping his son back on board. "But we will no' be in the boat with you, rather my son and I will be guiding you through the water."

"If we hurry, da'," the man whispered.

"Aye," he looked over his shoulder to the gathering storm. "Please. Though you donnae ken who we are, we are no' a threat to you. Can you trust us to get you to Skye and then to Erin?"

"You take us the whole way?" Aedan asked.

"We do," he nodded. "At Dagda's request. Come on board now."

Aedan nodded when Tristan looked at him, then helped his alpha on board. Weylyn locked eyes with his son before he boarded, and Aedan slipped a knife into his father's hands without anyone seeing. The boat was small, no room to phase if needed. A knife would be enough. Sitting on either side of their alpha, they flanked him, Weylyn's weapon concealed but readily available.

Dagda took his place at the helm and the father and son Selkies dived into the water.

Chapter Two

Fortunately, their delay did not cause the storm to catch up with them. It stayed well behind the boat as they sailed across the sea. Stopping at Skye for food and water, they continued south for another half-day until they arrived at a port in the northern tip of Erin. The Selkies did not leave the water, but Dagda and Aedan pulled the boat in further, allowing Weylyn and Tristan to come ashore. Dagda then let the ropes go and watched the boat drift towards his friends. The father and son swung on board in their human forms and waved, manning the boat and heading north.

Once they were out of sight, Dagda walked over to Aedan and stood eye to eye with him.

"Let me be perfectly clear," he started, his voice low and powerful. "This is my land and these are my people. If I state they are friends, you will not contradict me and you will not force them to reveal themselves, am I clear?"

"I will nae agree," Aedan replied. "'Tis clear to me you have never had to worry about the safety of your entire clan, the health and protection of your leader, and the pain of sending men to their deaths in war. I am War Chief and if I decide to question you and your motives then I will. I will nae undermine you so long as you keep me and my Alpha informed. These may be your people, but I protect *my* people and my Alpha. Donnae forget who I am, and I will nae forget who you are. We are allies but I donnae trust you."

"I do not need your trust, Aedan," Dagda answered. "But there are more things on this land than you have ever seen and there are things only I will know how to deal with."

"Then lead us," Tristan stepped forward. "I trust you and invoke your care of Caylean to lead us to him before it is too late. There is a strain of my father in him and I fear for his sanity now he has given up his mate."

"Aye," Weylyn replied. "I see it as well. We must get to him soon."

"When he was with me, he had his unrequited love of Giorsal to keep him grounded. Now..." Dagda's voice trailed off. "Let us go. I feel he has landed. My land is on the opposite side of Erin. Near the Kingdom of Duibhlinn, but we may run into many foes. I will have your pledge before we continue that you will listen and obey me should the need arise."

"You have it," Tristan answered. When his pack looked at him, he continued. "If and when the need may arise, we will listen to you."

Dagda nodded and they gathered their weapons and food. Weylyn looked back across the sea and took a deep breath. "We are safe, my love." He whispered. Aedan placed a hand on his father's shoulder.

"Are you well?" he asked.

"I am worried for my mate," Weylyn admitted. "The pup is due any day."

"She will be well," he answered. "But I do understand your fear. Phase if you desire and tell Blane we are well. We can wait."

Weylyn nodded and looked at the others who were gathering their things. Quickly, he phased and searched for Blane's conscious. He was sparing with one of Tristan's younger pups teaching him a new move. Once he was finished, Weylyn made himself known and asked to speak with his mate.

Of course, Blane replied and told the pup to wait for him as he searched for Eithne. The women were at the burn washing the clothes, when Weylyn saw Eithne through Blane's eyes. She was standing, stretching her back, and caressing her stomach.

"Blane," she smiled seeing him half-phased.

"Weylyn wished to speak with you," Blane said.

"Oh, thank the gods," she replied and looked up into Blane's eyes. "My love, are you well?"

Aye, dearest, Weylyn said and Blane spoke the words to her. *We have crossed to Erin. Dagda said Caylean is here. He can feel him, so can I. My love, are you all right?*

"Aye," she answered. "Donnae worry over me. I will be well and ask Blane to tell you when the pup is coming."

I should nae have left you, he shook his head. *'Tis no' good for you and I worry constantly.*

"You must no'," she replied with a smile. "I am well and have Isla and Labhaoise here with me. You concentrate on getting Caylean home safely."

How is Labhaoise?

"She is well. She and Bowdyn have stayed in their room today, but he says she is well."

Good, 'tis glad I am.

"Da'," Aedan called. "We should be going."

I must go now, love. I will try to speak with you again soon.

"I love you, Weylyn," she said. "Please be careful and come home to me in one piece."

I will. I love you too. Blane, please contact me when Eithne whelps.

I shall, he promised. *Fear no' for your mate, my friend. Odara and I will look after her and your new pup until you return.*

Thank you. He took one last long look at his mate and severed the connection with Blane by phasing back to his human form.

"Thank you for giving me a moment," he said to the others. "I needed to see my mate."

"Is she well?" Tristan asked.

"Aye," he replied.

"I am sorry you had to be away from your mate at this time," Dagda said. "But I promise you, we will get you back soon."

Eithne bit back her cry when Blane phased back into his human form essentially severing the connection with her husband. Blane's kind eyes met hers and he nodded.

"Donnae fear, Eithne," he said. "Weylyn will return soon. Until then, I promised him I would protect you."

"I thank you, Blane," she said. "I merely miss him and worry for him."

"Donnae worry," Blane replied. "Though I ken little of what you all are, I ken one thing, whatever it is, he will be well."

Eithne looked away from his searching eyes and nodded. The secret of their immortality was well kept but in the nearly thirty years Blane had been with them, none of them had aged. At that moment, her child moved within her and she smiled.

Forgive me, little one. I never wanted to sacrifice you. I hope you ken how much I love you. Your father and I love you.

Her baby kicked and moved around again, she smiled once more and stroked her protruding belly.

"Are you well, sister?" Isla slipped her hand through her arm.

"Aye," she answered. "The males have landed in Erin."

"Oh, thank the gods. But I meant you. You seemed sad."

"Merely thinking of Weylyn and how much we want this child."

"He loves you," Isla said as they walked together. "I have never seen him so happy."

"Ever?" Eithne asked.

"Of course," Isla stopped and turned to her. "Why do you ask such a question?"

She shrugged but Isla said nothing, waiting. "I suppose," Eithne started. "I still sometimes worry if I am enough. He loved Brietta so much... ignore me, it is pregnancy. I will be well."

Chapter Three

Weylyn carried the skin of water as he, Tristan, and Aedan followed Dagda through the woods. The green of the land was so vivid, none of them had ever seen anything as beautiful. Dagda moved with sure steps, pausing occasionally to listen. Finally, after several hours, he stopped.

"We stop here for the night. It is waning fast," he said.

"We should keep moving," Tristan replied. "We are all wolves, night means little to us."

"Aye," Dagda conceded. "But there is more than the darkness to worry over."

"Meaning what?" Aedan asked.

"Meaning we wait here and continue in the morning," Dagda stated.

Weylyn stepped forward when he saw Aedan move to argue.

"Thank you, Dagda. I find I am tired," Weylyn said. "Let us hunt for food."

Aedan offered to get them something. As Tristan and Weylyn started to set up camp and gather wood for a fire, they watched Dagda move about the four corners of the camp mumbling spells and using his hands, creating a protective barrier around them.

"As much as I believe his motives are good," Tristan whispered. "I donnae trust him."

"I understand, but we need his help," Weylyn stated. "He wants to find Caylean as much as we do."

Tristan fell silent as Dagda walked near to them.

"Do ye ken where he is, Dagda?" Weylyn called.

"I have a feeling," he answered. "He was going to my grove but now... we will see my father and he will perform a locator spell to be sure."

"Why do you no' do it?" Tristan asked.

"Not all druids have the power. It is a powerful spell, one I never learnt. I always had my senses to guide me, I never had need of it."

"When will we meet your father?" Weylyn asked.

"We should arrive in five days' time," Dagda replied.

Aedan entered the camp carrying a red deer over his shoulders.

"Does he expect us?" Aedan asked, his enhanced wolf hearing having caught the conversation.

"Nay, but I am sure it will be fine," Dagda replied. "We should eat and rest. There is no need for any guards. The wards are up. No one will be able to see us."

After they ate, the men stretched out near enough to the fire but far enough to hear anything in the woods. Something caught Tristan's ear, giggling. Seeing Weylyn's eyes wide awake, he questioned if he had heard it too. Weylyn nodded once and looked over at Aedan, his eyes constantly searching the darkness.

"Go to sleep," they heard Dagda say softly. "They will not bother you so long as you ignore them."

"What are they?" Tristan asked.

"Sprites. Fairies," Dagda replied. "We are four males travelling with no females. They are talking about us. Do not listen. They desire males and if you listen, they can bend you to their will and you will never return. Now, I say again, go to sleep and ignore them. Think only of your mates."

Nodding, Tristan, Aedan, and Weylyn settled in and went to sleep.

"Tristan," Alexina called to him. "Tristan," she softly kissed him awake.

"Mm," he groaned. "Alex? What are you doing here?" He woke seeing her over him, a bright smile on her face.

"There is my handsome mate," she said. "I love you."

"I love you," he replied. "What—"

"Shh," she stopped him. "Come with me. I need you."

"What is it?"

She raised his hand to her bare breast and tossed her head back letting out a sigh of ecstasy.

"Make me yours," she begged. "I ache for you, husband. Ease my need?"

She stood, forcing him to stand too as she kept his hand

firmly on her chest. Leading him away from the camp and further into the woods, she kept her hand over his.

"Where are we going?"

She turned suddenly and put a finger to his lips. Raising his other hand, she rubbed it against her chest and slowly lowered her hand to the front of his trousers.

"Alex," he breathed.

"Do you want me, husband?" she asked, leaning forward and kissing his neck.

"Aye, always," he groaned. "But…"

"Nay, come with me," she whispered.

"Tristan, nay," Dagda's voice broke through the lustful haze. "It is not Alexina before you. Shake away your lust. You must stop this."

He looked back at Dagda then to Alexina before him. Her image blurred and for a moment, he saw someone else. But then Alexina's face came to him again and she leaned forward, licking a line from his ear to the base of his throat, eliciting a groan from him.

"Nay, Tristan," Dagda's voice came again. "You know she is not real, or you would not have let me in. She is a Sprite, a Fae. She is not Alexina. She has you under her spell. Listen to my voice and come back. If you do not, you will never see Alexina again." Tristan's eyes turned back to Dagda. "You know I am right."

Looking back at Alexina, her image blurred, and a woman stood before him. Seeing her, he took a step back. She looked at Dagda and screamed. Her beautiful face turning monstrous. Her once vibrant brown hair turned grey and her face wrinkled and rotted. She screamed and raised her hand as if to grab Tristan, but Dagda grasped his arm and pulled him back, away from the slashing claws of the hellion before him. Dagda forced Tristan to look at him.

"We are in your mind, you must wake. I have no power here. Wake!"

The woman screamed again and raced to him just as Tristan shut his eyes. Opening them once more, he saw Weylyn and Aedan standing next to him and Dagda holding his head as if manipulating his thoughts.

"He is awake," Weylyn said.

"Thank the gods," Aedan replied, sheathing his dirk.

Dagda released him and Tristan sat up, groaning at the strain.

"What in the name of the gods happened?" Tristan asked.

"You listened to the Sprites," Dagda explained. "They nearly succeeded in drawing you to the Fae World. I have no power there. It was your strength that pulled you out."

"I thank you for your assistance. But how did you ken?" Tristan asked.

"We woke hearing the laughter again," Weylyn explained. "But when you did nae wake, Dagda kenned something was no' right."

"Thank you," he said. "Be wary. She came to me in Alexina's form."

"The sun is up. Let us break our fast a move on. This is only one of the perils that await us here in Erin," Dagda explained.

Chapter Four

"My dearest," Alexina said, softly stroking her daughter's arm. "You must eat," Giorsal, for three days, wept, waiting and hoping Caylean would return. For the last two days, she stood on the battlements looking out toward their boulder and the water beyond. She knew she should help the others restore the village after the attack, but she could not bring herself to do anything but wait for her mate's return.

"Giorsal," her mother urged.

"Thank you, Mama," she said. "But I am no' hungry."

"You must eat, for your child's sake," she replied. "Just a little something."

Debating, she had skipped far too many meals over the last few days. The last thing, she desired was to lose her child. If Caylean did not return, his child was all she had of him. Not remembering when last she ate, she acquiesced and walked with her mother to the Great Hall.

The druids who accompanied Dagda stayed on to assist with restoring the keep and bailey. The druid in charge stepped up to them.

"Are you well?" Agora asked.

"As well as I can be," Giorsal said.

"'Tis glad I am your mother convinced you to eat," she smiled softly. "Your child will need his sustenance."

"His?" Giorsal looked up. "You ken 'tis male?"

"Forgive me, I did not mean to give false hope," Agora said. "I merely meant... never mind."

"'Tis all right," Giorsal sighed. "Whatever it is, Caylean and I... I will be most grateful."

"Do not fear, child," Agora said. "Dagda looks upon Caylean as a son, he will not allow him to leave you."

Giorsal nodded but turned to her mother, "may I have a moment alone?" she asked.

"Of course, dearest one," Alexina said and took her leave, finding their cook and asking to lay the food.

"May I ask you something?" Giorsal said to Agora.

"Anything," the druid replied.

"You kenned Caylean over the sea in Erin, aye?" Giorsal asked.

"I did," she answered.

"Did you... that is... my mate has told me of your grove's... proclivities. Did you and Caylean—"

"Oh, no! Heavens, no, child," Agora calmed her. "The

gods have given me someone I care deeply for. We are not free to choose a mate or to mate but the gods are merciful, and they have only decreed us to be... with each other. There have been times when he was needed to prove his worth with another, but it is very few. We have had an arrangement for several years. Caylean, though not with me, was called upon, but I was told he only thought of you. He tried to speak to the gods begging them to release him but when they would not, he looked upon it as a chore, something to be endured, not enjoyed. He has left to protect you. Though I know it gives you no comfort, he has always wanted to protect you."

"He has returned to your grove, breaking his promise to me. How is that protecting me?" Giorsal demanded.

Agora took a deep breath before she answered. "It is what he knows," she explained. "It is where he believes he belongs."

"He belongs with me," Giorsal snapped.

"Aye and that is what Dagda has gone to tell him," Agora soothed. "But now come."

After a moment, Giorsal went on, "'tis Dagda, is it no'?"

"What is?" Agora questioned.

"The one you love. The one the gods gave you."

Agora looked down, but then smiled and locked eyes with her.

"Come now, let us get you something to eat," she said taking her arm and guiding her to the *dais* where her mother, Isla, and Eithne waited.

The wolves had followed Dagda for four more days, all remembering their promise to him to listen should the need arise. After the attack on Tristan by the Woodland Sprite, they had agreed to alternate keeping watch. It had been an uneventful evening so far, as they all remained quiet around the fire. The mutton sizzled and popped over the open flame.

"How much longer to your father, Dagda?" Weylyn finally asked.

"We should be there in a day," Dagda replied. "But there are things between us and him that could make the crossing difficult. Vikings still inhabit this area, not to mention the *Fir Bolg* and *Tuatha Dé Danann.*"

"You have strange beliefs here in Erin," Aedan shook his head.

"And you do not in Scotland?" Dagda asked.

"What is *Scotland?*" Weylyn questioned.

"Alba," Dagda corrected. "It will be known as Scotland soon."

"And you ken this, how?" Weylyn asked.

"I have many talents," Dagda replied. "Such as..." He waved his hand and a bottle appeared. "Would anyone care for a swig of whisky?"

"A what?" They asked together.

"A drink," he clarified, offering the whisky to Tristan.

"You and my grandson speak differently than the rest of us," Weylyn said, accepting the flagon from Tristan after he drank.

"We do," Dagda replied simply.

"Is there a reason?" Aedan asked.

"There is," Dagda answered but did not elaborate.

After a moment, Tristan shook his head and sighed.

"I donnae understand you, my friend," he said.

"Perhaps one day," Dagda smiled for the first time and the sight surprised the wolves.

"Can you tell me how you received your scar?" Aedan

asked as he took a drink.

Dagda sobered a moment. "It was in battle," he started. "My grove was betrayed, and we were at battle with Romans. Geileis, as you already know, was someone I cared deeply for. She married my younger brother; Flynn. He was troubled. He stole – or she did 'tis not clear – Lucien's Dagger. He had killed several of my kin before I had a chance to stop him. This," he indicated the scar marring his face, "was from him."

"What happened to him?" Aedan asked.

"He died," Dagda replied and took a long draw from the whisky.

The fire crackled and popped as they sat in silence. Weylyn sighed and stood. "I will take the first watch. Get some rest."

"Wake me when you need to be relieved," Aedan offered. "I will take over."

"My thanks," Weylyn smiled at his son, grateful for the thousandth time Caylean was able to heal him.

Stepping away from the group, Weylyn took up his post at the old oak tree and half-phased. Blane popped into his head.

Is all well? Weylyn immediately asked.

Och aye, Blane answered. *Is Tristan there?*

Aye, he is at camp, Weylyn explained.

Alexina asked me to tell him, Giorsal is better. She spoke to one of the druid women who accompanied Dagda and she set her fears at ease. Giorsal, though still mourning, has become much more her old self.

Thank the gods, Weylyn sighed. *How is Eithne?*

She is well and beginning to prepare for your pup's arrival. But she did ask me to tell you, if you phased, she loves you and to tell you she was remembering the day of the storm. She said you would ken what that means, Blane explained.

Weylyn grinned but was careful not to reveal what that meant. Blane did not need to know intimate details.

Tell her, if you would, remembering is all well and good but no' without me.

Blane chuckled. *I will, my friend. Be well.* Blane shifted back to his human form, severing the connection between them.

Weylyn leaned up against the tree and took a deep breath. Eithne reminded him of when they mated during the fiercest snowstorm they had ever seen.

His mind drifting, he did not hear the movement beside him, until the knife was thrown, slicing through the fleshy part of his shoulder. Crying out, he pressed a hand to the wound, his fingers straddling the knife, still protruding from his flesh. A battle cry went up around him as he hurried back to the camp.

"*Dùisg!*" Weylyn shouted for them to wake.

The wolves were on their feet immediately. Aedan's eyes found his father and the wound. The three surrounded Weylyn as they grasped their weapons and half-phased. Men emerged from the woods shouting and running toward them.

Seeing it was easily five-to-one and that was if Weylyn could fight, Aedan's mind tried to calculate what to do. No time to think, swords clashed against each other's and Dagda's spells would not work. Something or someone had placed a barrier spell around them. Throwing Tristan another sword when his was knocked out of his hand, Aedan felled several warriors but there were too many of them. Weylyn fought with them but his strength was failing. His concentration on his father as Weylyn fell to his knees, a warrior standing over him, their swords crossed, Aedan did not deflect a blow and he felt the cut to his left thigh.

Falling to the ground on one knee, Aedan took the lower height to his advantage and sliced through the man's stomach.

When Tristan received a blow, Aedan knew it was over. The fighting slowly stopped, and the warriors stood over them.

One man, holding a sword to Tristan's throat, said something in a foreign language. Tristan looked around but did not answer.

Hearing Dagda speak in low tones, the man's gaze flew to him. He spoke loudly as he approached Dagda, murder in his eyes. Dagda answered him calmly in the same language, but it did not seem to stop the man. He sliced slowly over Dagda's left arm. The dark druid did not cry out. He stared the man down even as his flesh tore and his blood spilled. Without preamble, the warrior screamed in his face and raised the sword to take his head.

Suddenly, one of the men screamed and was pulled into the darkness. The leader looked up sharply and lowered his sword. Another man screamed and was pulled away. Then another and another until the leader was alone. He raised his sword, shaking with fear. His wild eyes scanned the woods looking for whatever demon took his men. Then, they all heard it. The leader paled and turned around. The glowing eyes were the first thing they saw. The leader dropped his sword as a black bear, the largest the wolves had ever seen, materialized out of the woods, slowly stalking toward the leader.

The leader stuttered but said nothing intelligible until he let out a scream. The bear rushed forward; his strong jaw clamped around the man's leg. The leader's screams haunted the wolves as the bear dragged him into the woods. When they were alone, Weylyn groaned and fell to his knees. Aedan hobbled to his father and checked the wound. Tristan hurried to them both, a bruise forming on the side of his head where one of the warriors struck him with the hilt of a sword.

Dagda stood before them, his eyes scanning the woods. When the leader's screams stopped, all eyes turned to the darkness. The bear roared and appeared before them again. The attack was coming.

Suddenly, Dagda raised his hand and in a commanding voice, spoke, "Rhydian, calm."

The bear looked at him, then to the wolves.

"Rhydian, I said calm," he spoke again.

The bear again looked at him, rose to his hind legs, then started to shake. The beast collapsed in a heap and instead of the black fur, a male with blonde hair looked up from the ground.

"Dagda?" he questioned.

"Aye, brother," Dagda replied and helped him up, slipping his cloak around his naked form. "'Tis glad we are you chose that moment to approach."

"I saw him cut you," the male said. "Are you well?"

"Aye," Dagda clapped him on the shoulder. "How are you? How is Delia? And my nephew?"

"All well. Delia had a vision of you and sent me here," the male said. "Striken wanted to join me but we both said nay."

"'Tis well he did not. You had things well in hand, Rhydian."

"No' to interrupt," Aedan's annoyed voice spoke. "But both my father and I are bleeding, Druid."

Dagda turned to look back and then, with a nod to Rhydian, he walked over to Weylyn and Aedan. The barrier had been lifted when the leader was killed, and Dagda successfully healed them both. Rhydian stepped into the camp and waited. Dagda turned with the wolves.

"Rhydian, this is Tristan, Alpha of the Loch Alsh Pack and his Beta and War Chief," Dagda introduced.

"I watched you fight," Rhydian's deep timbered voice was not surprising from the much taller man. "You all did well."

"Who were those men?" Aedan demanded.

"Celts," Rhydian stated. "Slaves of Biróg."

"Biróg?" Dagda questioned.

"Aye, she has not given up her pursuit of us. I suppose she sensed you. Fortunately, the cloaking spell both Delia and your father cast over our cottage has held and even the *Tuatha Dé Danann* cannot find us."

"You speak a different language," Aedan grumbled.

"All you need to know is, my father and sister are two of the most powerful druids. There was an encounter with another powerful druid and my father refused whatever it is she demanded. Rhydian is my brother-by-marriage. I called to my sister when I knew we were outnumbered," Dagda explained.

"I am only sorry you were caught in this fight," Rhydian said. "Please, come with me. Delia will want to know you are well and she is a definitive cook."

"We need to find Caylean," Weylyn spoke softly.

"Aye, but I do believe we will accept your most generous offer," Tristan spoke to Rhydian. The blonde man smiled and beckoned them to follow.

About a league away, they came upon a clearing and Rhydian whistled. The protective shield waivered before them and the wards lowered, revealing a cottage with smoke coming from the chimney. Rhydian crossed and held the gate open for them. As soon as the gate closed, the protection lowered again.

The door opened and a woman and young boy greeted them. The woman looked over at Dagda and raced to him. Embracing tightly, it was not difficult for the wolves to see the familial resemblance. Both Dagda and the female had dark blonde hair but instead of Dagda's brown eyes, she had blue.

"'Tis glad I am to see you, brother," she said. "I feared for you greatly."

"I am well, sister," Dagda replied. "I thank you for hearing my call for assistance."

"She went into a trance," the young man with dark blonde hair, no older than the human age of sixteen, said beside her. "Told me to get da'."

"'Tis glad we are," Dagda said, embracing the young

man.

"Dagda, do introduce us," she smiled, indicating the wolves.

"If you will forgive me," Rhydian said. "I will go dress."

Delia nodded to her husband as he passed her and placed a kiss on her lips. Dagda took his sister's hand and turned to his traveling companions.

"Delia, this is Tristan, Alpha of the Loch Alsh Pack and his Beta and War Chief," Dagda stated. "My sister and nephew, Bedelia and Striken."

"A pleasure to meet you, my lady," Tristan bowed his head toward her. "Forgive our appearance. As you ken, we were in a fight."

Her face fell and she looked down. "I am sorry you were drawn into our fight."

"Nae trouble, my lady," Tristan replied.

"Come in. I have some hearty stew ready," she ushered everyone through and welcomed them to their cottage.

It was larger than it appeared with a common area and two sides leading to two bedrooms. Rhydian appeared through one of the hallways, dressed in a tan tunic and leggings. His blonde hair hung long below his shoulders and his full beard, of the same color, was neatly brushed.

Soon, they sat together and ate in relative silence. The young male kept eyeing Aedan with avid curiosity. Aedan finally turned to him and smiled.

"Ask what it is you wish to ask, lad," Aedan said.

All eyes turned to Striken who looked down, as his pale face reddened. "Forgive me," he said. "I find you fascinating. I have never met a War Chief before."

"'Tis something the lad has been interested in, almost since he was in his mother's womb," Rhydian replied.

"'Tis an honorable profession," Aedan said. "I have been most fortunate to serve two great leaders."

"How long did you train?" he asked.

"I had been learning to fight since my mother's husband, a man I looked up to as my father before I kenned of my true parentage, helped teach me. He was in our chief's guard. Shieling, the chief, was ten years my senior but he was watching the men spar one day. I was twenty-one and my father had me join him training in the bailey. Shieling watched me and when I defeated my father, he applauded and asked to spar with me and made me swear not to let him win. When he won by just a breath, he invited me to dine with him. During dinner, he gave me scenarios asking what I would do if faced with them. Afterward, he walked with me home and asked if I would be amenable to becoming his War Chief, a position which had been vacated by the untimely death of my predecessor from a raid. I agreed and for nearly twenty years I served proudly by his side."

"We have no chief, but it is something I have always wished to be, but all human villages have wolf's bane and I cannot be around that," Striken said.

"Why?" Tristan asked.

"I hold to my grandfather's linage. I phase as a wolf not a bear," he explained.

"My affliction is from my father, my mother was a druid," Rhydian explained.

"And though the wolf is dormant within me, it was passed to my son," Delia stated.

"Aedan is a great asset to my leadership," Tristan replied. "I would be lost without his father and him. But I fear we must be on our way. We need to find Caylean."

"My father is very near," Dagda replied standing. "I am sorry to dash, sister but I feel the urgency to find him."

"Of course, perhaps you will join us on the way back?" she offered.

"'Twould be our honor," Tristan said. "We thank you, most ardently for your hospitality and of course, most of all, saving our lives."

"It was our pleasure," Delia stated. "Rhydian will walk with you to our father's house."

"There is no need, sister," Dagda replied. "Now that Biróg's spell is lifted, I have possession of all of my powers. We are well."

"I was not asking, brother," Delia said in a manner that made the wolves nearly laugh. She was clearly the younger sister, but she ordered Dagda around as if she was older.

Rhydian's hand landed on Dagda's shoulder and, with a chuckle, he spoke, "in all these years of marriage, Dagda I have learned to never question my wife. I join you."

"My husband knows me well," Delia smiled in triumph.

"Aye, fine, Rhydian travels with us," Dagda acquiesced.

His sister and nephew followed them to the gate where Delia lifted the wards and bade them farewell.

Everyone walked in silence for a while before Weylyn eventually spoke, "Rhydian," he called to the man walking with Dagda.

"Aye?" the Bearman answered.

"You said you change due to your father, but you look like one of the Viking Invaders. How old are you?"

"You are correct," he replied. "My father was a Viking, and my mother was a druid. I am what is termed a hybrid. I lived for a while on Skye, my father called the isle home for decades before he met my mother. That is where I met Delia. As for how old I am, well I will say I am younger than Dagda." He slapped his brother-in-law on the shoulder. Dagda chuckled.

"Aye and you all know I am not young," Dagda replied.

They fell silent again and walked on. Finally, Rhydian stopped, a mountain looming before them.

"This is where I leave you," Rhydian said.

"You are not joining us?" Dagda asked.

"Nay," Rhydian chuckled. "Your father still intimidates me."

Dagda laughed once. "Aye, he does that well. Be well, Rhydian."

Dagda offered his arm in a warrior's shake. Rhydian took it and pulled him into an embrace.

"Be well, Dag," he said. "Come by with that lovely lady of yours soon."

"She is not mine," Dagda replied.

"Aye, keep telling yourself that," Rhydian grinned and turned to the wolves. "Good luck looking for your lad. Caylean is a good male."

"We thank you for your timely deliverance," Tristan stated.

Rhydian waved him off and headed back across the path before phasing into his bear form and bounding back to his family.

The wolves looked to Dagda who indicated the mountain. "Come and meet my father."

They started up the mountain just as the storm that threatened all day, released its downpour. By the time they reached a small platform at the mouth of a cave, they were drenched through.

"How much further, Druid?" Aedan called.

"We are here," Dagda replied and faced the entrance. He spoke in a loud clear voice, a language the wolves had never heard before. The cave's entrance glimmered in the rain and revealed two sentries beside the entrance, their swords poised to attack. Tristan, Aedan, and Weylyn half-phased ready to defend themselves.

The druid warriors growled at the wolves who snarled in response.

"Enough!" a man shouted from inside the cave. The druids lowered their swords but kept a wary eye on the wolves. The rain stopped immediately. Movement from inside the cave drew their gazes, the druids on either side pulled up to attention.

A man and woman appeared out of the darkness both similarly dressed in a long tunic, covered by a longer cloak. The woman's hair was in a long single braid, but the man drew their attention. His light brown hair hung to his mid back with two braids on either side of his temples. His eyes were a dark brown but what captivated them, was the blue ink in swirled designs on his forearms, neck and even across his eyes. He was a dark druid but Weylyn's suspicions were confirmed when he spoke.

"Dagda, 'tis good to see you, lad, but why have you brought the descendants of my nephew here?"

"Da' we need your help," Dagda replied with a bow.

"So, I see," he answered.

"We did not expect you until Samhain," the woman stepped forward and embraced him. "It is so good to see you, love."

"I have missed you, mum," he said. She passed a hand over his face and smiled softly then turned to the others. The man stared at Weylyn. Looking at his alpha and son, Weylyn looked away from the man's intense and questioning gaze.

"For shame, husband," she spoke. "They are all soaked through, bring them in."

"First, I need to know who they are," the man stated.

"Tristan, Weylyn, and Aedan, they journey with me,"

Dagda introduced.

"Aye, but *who* are they?" he stressed.

"I see you already ken who we are, Lord," Tristan replied. "I claim nae inheritance from Marrock apart from sirehood."

The man's lip curled in a growl and the two sentries raised their swords.

"Dagda," the woman said. "I do believe you should explain."

"Forgive me," he said. "We are needing da' assistance in finding Caylean."

"Caylean?" the woman asked surprised. "Is he well?"

"'Tis a long story," Dagda replied.

"He is my son," Aedan stepped forward.

"That would be true, since you are a half-breed and he a hybrid. My son has told me of his ward's sire," the man replied.

"May I ask who you are?" Weylyn questioned. The man's unnerving gaze returned to Weylyn.

"Of course, forgive me," the woman said. "I am Myrna, High Priestess and this is my husband."

Weylyn did not miss how she did not say his name. He decided to test his theory.

"You are Lucien," Weylyn stated. The two sentries poised for attack. The man raised his hand to them, but they only relaxed slightly.

"Why do you say that?" he asked.

"Only one with the power to take the life of an immortal would be so protected. Also, Dagda said he was the son of the first family. I have studied Lucien's Dagger my whole life. It was no' a far leap to make," Weylyn explained.

The two men stared at each other for a long moment,

then Lucien finally nodded. "Aye, wolf, I do not use my name. We have had others search for me in the past. But understand, I need no protection."

"I would believe it," Weylyn answered. "Were it no' for these." He indicated the two sentries.

"They keep the entrance, 'tis true," Myrna replied. "Please come in and let me get you something dry to wear."

One more look between Weylyn and Lucien and the wolves followed the woman inside. As soon as they were alone, Lucien stopped his son with a hand on his chest. Leaning close, he lowered his voice. "I expect answers."

"Aye," Dagda answered. "I will tell you whatever you ask later, but I beg you... We need to locate Caylean."

"You know you are always welcome, and they are your cousins, Alasdair's kin but I do not know who they are. Do you vouch for them?"

"Aye, I would never bring harm to you or mother," Dagda said.

"They are Marrock's kin," Lucien growled.

"Aye, but so are we. We have the same sire though many years removed."

"Marrock is no kin of ours. He took after your mother's father. The cruel tyrant who nearly killed your Aunt Deena."

"I know the story, da'," Dagda replied. "But I ask you to give them aid. I would never seek you nor reveal where you are, if I did not believe Caylean needed help. He gave up his mate."

Lucien took a deep breath. "I am sorry for the lad. Of course, I will help. I know how much you care for him."

"The gods have not given me permission to sire a son. Caylean is as close to a son as I have had in these many centuries."

Lucien cupped his son's jaw.

"I could beg an audience. Ask why."

"Nay," Dagda shook his head.

"You deserve to be happy. I have seen what losing Geileis did to you. It is time for you to love again."

"I will not ask that."

"Then come, I wish to help you, but I will speak no more on it until you ask."

Together they turned and headed into the cave.

The sights that greeted the wolves as they walked into the cave, took their breath away. After walking down a short corridor, the main area opened. Soaring ceilings carved out of the stone of the mountain and lined with wood panels. Wooden chandeliers with flickering flames illuminated the great banquet hall. The multiple levels lined the sides of the great hall and disappeared into the mountain, not to cut through the towering ceilings. A stone fireplace proudly displayed in the middle of the side wall, cut by roughly honed stone. A roaring fire was lit giving enough heat to warm the entire space.

Above the large mantle, was a crest of arms, an ancient one as Weylyn had never seen it before. Lucien clapped his hands once to get the attention from the servants around them.

"My son has returned," he spoke. "Let us celebrate and welcome our kith and kin." Turning to the wolves, he opened his arms in a welcoming gesture. "All are welcome here. Please join us for some food."

"We thank you," Tristan answered. "But is there perhaps a place we can dry off? We have nae wish to leave a water stain."

"Of course," Lucien began and with a wave of his hand, their clothes were instantly dry. The wolves looked at each other surprised, but Dagda stepped forward. "I ken you wish to speak with me, but perhaps it would be best done after dinner. You are all hungry and tired."

"Aye," Tristan agreed. "But we cannae stay long."

"You will stay and recover and until such time as you are fit for travel," Lucien said.

"We will leave as soon as we can," Tristan argued. Weylyn stepped forward and placed a hand on Tristan's shoulder.

"May I have a word, my alpha?" he asked. Tristan's eyes narrowed, but he nodded.

"Give us a moment," Tristan said as he turned from Lucien and stepped back with Weylyn and Aedan. "What is it?"

"You ken I wish to find Caylean as much as you, Tristan but I do believe we should take a moment and wait here at least for a day or two."

"And why do you say that?" Tristan asked.

"Because this is the first family, our family. Our ancestor's uncle. He would ken more about Caylean, since he is a hybrid and Lucien trained the first hybrid. I believe it would be prudent to speak with him. Stay with him and learn how to handle Caylean. Not only is he something none of us have dealt with in the past, but now he has given up his mate, he is unpredictable. I fear for him greatly." When Tristan did not respond, Weylyn went on. "Have I ever given you reason no' to trust me? Have I ever asked you for anything without having a legitimate reason?"

"Of course no'," Tristan shook his head. "But you must ken my reticence. Lucien is the only one who can kill us. And now he has his dagger again since Dagda took it from Geileis. I worry."

"Aye," Aedan replied. "I agree with Tristan, Da'. 'Tis no' safe. I donnae ken who he is and therefore I donnae ken how to protect us."

"You both have valid arguments," Weylyn went on. "But I have always followed my instincts. Something is drawing me here. To them. Something I cannae explain. I trust him. I believe we should stay at least one night in order to learn what we can about a Hybrid. That way we are more prepared for what lies ahead of us when we find Caylean. Trust me, Tristan. I am well aware of the risks, but I ken it is worth it."

Tristan was quiet for a long moment before he turned to Aedan. "What say you, War Chief?"

Aedan took a deep breath. "I trust my father. If he says we should stay, we should stay. But as your safety is foremost in my mind, I would suggest we all sleep in the same room and take turns keeping watch."

"If it would make you feel better," Dagda interrupted. The wolves turned to him. "My father and I have agreed to give you this." He produced the dagger they had only seen briefly when Geileis attempted to kill him. "If you have it, perhaps it would give you the peace you seek."

With Tristan's permission, Aedan stepped forward and accepted the dagger. "I thank you," he said looking at both Dagda and Lucien. "I hope you understand our reticence. We will keep this on our persons and give it back to you when we leave. We appreciate this gesture of trust. Please forgive us for our skepticism."

"No apology needed," Lucien replied, his eyes once more on Weylyn. "I do understand. Now, join us for dinner and we will speak more."

Chapter Six

Dinner was laid and as the wolves sat at the main table, Aedan's eyes never stopped moving. Even with Lucien's Dagger on his person, he was still wary. But he smiled and pretended for the time being. Tristan sat beside Lucien at the head of the table across from Dagda. Weylyn was between his alpha and his son but across from Myrna.

"Is the food not to your liking?" Myrna asked Weylyn as she raised the wine goblet to her lips.

"My apologies, my lady," Weylyn assured her. "'Tis just I have never eaten anything like this before. Might I ask, what is it?"

"The main ingredient here in Erin is potato. This dish is

called Shepherd's Pie. 'Tis made with lamb meat and the potato, after boiling, is mashed."

"'Tis very good, my lady," Aedan complimented as he dug into the meal.

"It caters to our wolf-selves," Tristan replied.

"It may surprise you to learn, Alpha, I am wolf kind as well," Lucien stated.

"We have seen Dagda's wolf. Since 'tis well kenned Myrna is a High Priestess, it could only be you who is wolf," Tristan answered.

Lucien looked over at his son, his dark eyes burning. Dagda locked eyes with his father, not backing down from his disciplinary look.

"It was necessary," Dagda replied.

"I am sure you weighed every option, darling," his mother said patting his hand and giving her husband a side glance.

Aedan looked between the father and son, then to his father. Leaning back from the table, he chuckled.

"I ken well that look, Dagda. Is it no' done? For you to phase? Your father seems most displeased."

"'Tis not something I usually need to do," Dagda replied. "Only when I need to cover a large amount of ground in a quick time but am not with other druids."

"Such as at the wedding of Gregor and Loeiza," Weylyn stated. They looked over at him. "My mate has the gift of foresight. She saw you arrive."

"The gift is only so long as a female remains a maiden." Myrna's eyes went to Aedan then back. "Are you saying she is still one?"

Weylyn shifted uncomfortably and cleared his throat. "Nay, my lady, she is no'. But she still has dreams and though the visions are no' as clear as before, she does still have them. The image she saw was of you and Lucien's dagger."

Dagda and Lucien leaned forward. "Did she tell you this vision?" Dagda asked.

"She did," Weylyn nodded.

"Tell us, if you would Beta. I am interested," Lucien stated.

"She had the vision a few years ago. It was disjointed but, she saw three cloaked figures walk up to Gregor's keep. These figures looked up and then a flash of Lucien's Dagger. We were courting at the time, so she was still..."

"A maiden?"

"Aye, then when we were celebrating with Gregor and Loeiza, she saw you and the other two arrive. She kenned it was the vision. Then with..." Weylyn looked at Tristan for his permission to continue sharing what happened within the pack. Tristan nodded once. "The second part of her vision came to pass when Geileis and Eion attempted to overthrow Tristan. She saw in a dream, someone close to us, betray us. She, we all thought it was my alpha's daughter's young man but when he died, she had the vision again. That is when we kenned it was someone else."

"Who?"

"My brother, Eion. We share the same sire, but my mother passed many years before and Marrock took another. Eion wanted to be alpha. He was much like our father," Tristan explained. "He used Geileis' hatred for Dagda and a druid named Liam Arc'hantael in the attempted overthrow of me."

"I know Liam Arc'hantael. His father was Gabhran who Marrock killed," Lucien said.

"Not killed. Bit. He became a male named Maelogan. For a time, he was part of our pack. Then he was my son's dear friend but only to keep an eye on him," Weylyn replied.

"He killed my mother," Aedan interjected.

"My first mate," Weylyn explained.

"Liam's mother, Gabhran's wife was killed by Marrock during a raid," Lucien said.

"That explains much," Tristan agreed.

"Eion and Liam plotted together and Geileis used the dagger and killed one of her sisters," Weylyn explained.

"For a short time," Dagda replied touching the new marking on his neck.

"Well," Lucien said abruptly and leaned back. "It is getting late. You are all tired."

Almost immediately, the wolves yawned and felt their eyes droop.

"Lucien," Myrna scolded. "For shame. Let them finish their meal."

The Dark Druid looked at his wife and nodded once. The tiredness disappeared.

"Please, eat," Myrna said and motioned for the serving women to fill their goblets of ale.

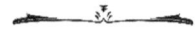

Eithne held a lantern as she walked through the darkened keep. The child was especially active at night and without Weylyn's calming touch, the child refused to settle. Stroking her belly, Eithne found a walk was the best way to calm both mother and child and to alleviate the ache in her ankles and calves.

As always, her mind drifted to Weylyn and the night they conceived their sixth child. A soft smile lifted the corners of her lips when she remembered his gentle yet commanding touch. She missed him.

"Eithne?" The sound of Bowdyn's voice behind her caused her to turn. Her brother by law, peoples and marriage trotted down the stairs. "Are you well?" he opened his arms to her, and she accepted his brotherly embrace.

"Aye," she said, taking in his scent, one of freshly cut wood and sun-bleached grass. She took a deep breath in. Since she mated Weylyn and every time she carried his child, her senses were heightened almost as a wolf. And as she expected, she sensed nothing, but goodness in Bowdyn and it made her smile.

"Are you sure?" he asked rubbing his hands up and down her arms. She nodded into his chest. After one more deep inhalation, she looked up at him.

"I miss my mate," she confided. "And our child is particularly active when he is no' here."

"I am sorry." He kissed her forehead. "I am sure he is well… Forgive me, but which one is he? I did nae get a chance to meet him properly."

"Weylyn," she replied. "And as for which one he is, he is the most handsome."

Bowdyn's face turned skeptical. "I ken I may be an intelligent man, my dear one, but even I draw the line at naming a man handsome."

Eithne giggled and nodded. "Aye, but 'twas enjoyable to see your reaction. My mate is the more… mature one of the three. He is the Beta wolf. And Aedan's father."

"Ah, I see," Bowdyn replied. "I do see by the twinkle in your eyes you find him handsome."

"He is and he is my soulmate."

"Are you happy?"

"Very."

"Good. Else, I would need to speak with him."

She laughed again but heard another voice behind them.

"Oh, I am sorry, my dears. I wondered where you went, Bowdyn," Labhaoise said still standing on the stairs.

"Merely to get more water, my love," Bowdyn walked over to her and took her in his arms. A pang of sadness hit Eithne's heart, it would be the first birth where Weylyn was not by her side. Still, it was a joyous moment to see her sister alive and well.

"But you ambushed poor Eithne instead," Labhaoise teased with a wide grin.

"I had no' spoken to her about her husband and needed to do so," he laughed.

"Ever the vigilant elder brother to my sister," Labhaoise loving touched his chest.

"Of course," he answered pushing her light brown hair away from her eyes. "I take care of my women."

"You do indeed," Labhaoise replied in a low tone. Eithne laughed at Bowdyn's blush but offered to get the water for them and promptly excused herself.

It was dark as Eithne approached the kitchens. Her lantern cast a low glow over the flagstone floor. An eerie feeling grew in the pit of her stomach. She hurried over to the table where a pitcher of water sat. Setting her lantern down, she reached for the pitcher, when a soft noise came from the larder. Eithne froze. Cook did not sleep in the larder; she had her own chambers above stairs with her maid. Slowly taking the lantern, she walked over to the heavy oak door.

Raising the lantern, she reached for the handle when the sound happened again but louder. Eithne jumped back and the lantern flickered, and the flame went out, no oil left.

Bathed in darkness, Eithne tried to calm her heartrate and breathing. Something was wrong. After a moment, her eyes adjusted to the darkness. Still unable to see as well as she would have hoped, she reached for the door and, after a fortifying breath, she opened it and screamed.

Bowdyn took off running. He reached the pitch-black

kitchen hearing Eithne scream again. Immediately, he shouted a spell that illuminated the room. Seeing Eithne fighting the air, he rushed to her and forced her to look at him. He sensed the dark magic coming from the larder. Someone had created a trap, something darker than he had dealt with in the past had fallen on her. Dispelling the residual less powerful evil, Bowdyn forced Eithne to look at him. Finally, Eithne's unfocused eyes fell on his.

"You are safe," his commanding voice echoed in the empty space. Eithne breathed deeply and nodded but then her eyes widened, and she bent over clutching her stomach, crying out as a rush of water escaped between her legs.

Bowdyn took a step back looking at her in astonishment.

"The child," she groaned. "Is coming now."

Chapter Seven

Dagda walked into the great hall to see his father standing by the fire. Lucien turned and smiled slightly, offering his son a glass of whiskey. Dagda accepted the drink and they stood together before the fire, not speaking.

Finally, Lucien broke the silence. "You have yet to heal your eye, I see."

Dagda sighed. "It is my penance, a constant reminder."

"Flynn was going to kill you, then me, then your mother," Lucien said. "You did what you had to do. You cannot live in the past."

"It does not stop the fact, I killed my own brother," Dagda replied.

"He was always troubled. Being half human bothered him more than any of us expected."

"He found out his father could be one of many Romans who kidnapped and raped his mother. That would affect anyone, especially a male who always felt different."

"I never treated him any differently than you or your sister. Flynn was my son as well, even if it was nae by blood," Lucien replied. Dagda's ears tuned to his father's rare Highland accent indicative of where he was born as a human.

"And you always did. I am not blaming you, Da'," Dagda said. "I only wish there had been another way. Flynn left Geileis behind and she blames me. I... found out it was she who gave him the dagger. She stole it from you."

Lucien took a drink of his whiskey. "Aye, I ken that, lad," he replied. Dagda stared at his father.

"Why did you not tell me?"

"You were so in love with her and Flynn was no' well," Lucien explained. "No one should ever learn that about their sire, nor the horror their mother went through."

"I would have hoped he would see you as the man who took him as his own. Someone who cared for him even though you did not need to. That is the man I honor and respect as my sire."

"You ken I love your mother, nae matter what horrors she went through. She is as strong as an oak. Her children are mine, nae matter who sired them. But Flynn took it poorly and I believe it was his backward desire to meet his father that caused him to turn against us," Lucien sighed. "I should have told him. He should not have found out from Bírog."

"You did what you did to protect him and mother. It was not your fault."

"When you have a son of your own, you will understand," Lucien said.

Dagda took a drink and paused. "That is not in the gods' plans for me."

"You ken this for certs?" Lucien asked.

"They have not made anything clear apart from the fact they desire me to prove my loyalty."

"And with whom have you proved your loyalty? Is it not Agora for the last several decades? Or is it a century?"

"She is forever marked because we allowed our feelings to guide us into each other's arms instead of listening to the gods' will."

"Donnae give me that, lad. You took the mark as your own. Do not think I have not seen all your markings and ken what each one means... Do you love her?"

"Of course, I do," he answered. "But I am unable to act upon it."

"And yet the gods have not asked you to be with anyone else but her?"

"Aye, only once with Kyriea to teach Caylean—"

"And have the gods asked Agora to be with anyone else but you?"

"Nay but—"

"That seems a clear message to me, lad," he said. Lucien held up a hand to prevent him from saying anything. "I will leave it for now. But perhaps pray about it. Your mother and I pray for you and your sister, constantly."

"We met Delia on the way here," Dagda replied. "She is well and asked me to send Striken's and her love. Rhydian was supposed to join us, but he claims you still intimidate him."

"Good," Lucien answered then cracked a smile. "Your mother and I do not get to visit as often as we would like, but we will see them soon."

"What are my lads discussing?" Myrna's voice came

from the stairs. The men turned and greeted her with a kiss when she approached.

"We were just speaking about Delia, Rhydian, and Striken," Dagda said.

Lucien sat at one of the armchairs and pulled his wife down on his lap. "Rhydian is still intimidated by me."

"You seem far too happy about that," she lightly slapped his chest.

"'Tis a father's prerogative." He grinned and kissed her neck. "Are our guests comfortable?" He pulled back.

"Aye, I was finally able to convince them that with the dagger, no one would murder them in their beds. They agreed to separate chambers."

"They are a suspicious lot," Lucien said.

"As are we."

"Aye," Lucien then turned to his son. "What happened with Caylean? Why did he leave?"

"He is a hybrid," Dagda revealed. "But he is unlike any I have seen. He stans as a man on wolf legs, his eyes black and yellow. His change was triggered when he saw his mate attacked. Then later still, it appeared he was in control, but he was struck by an arrow tipped with wolf's bane. When his mother carried him early in her womb, she drew out the wolf's bane poison from Tristan, and in doing so, Caylean created an immunity to it. It did not hurt him, it made him stronger. He attacked his father. Nearly killing him. Afraid of hurting his mate, he ran, not speaking with me first. I worry about him."

Lucien nodded sagely. "He has far too much evil in him. He tries to suppress it, but I fear, unchecked and without his mate to ground him, he could become far worse than Marrock."

"I sense it too," Dagda agreed. "He blocked me out with more power than I thought him capable of. He is strong."

"Aye," Lucien replied. "We will perform the locator spell,

but surely you ken where he is."

"I?" Dagda asked surprised. "Nay, I do not."

"Where did he feel most comfortable? Where was he not an outsider? Think, lad, you ken where he is."

"I thought he would return to my grove. But surely my people would have told me by now."

"Unless he commanded them not to, or perhaps he has not made up his mind and still wanders."

"We will know for certain when you perform the spell, my love," Myrna said. "I will begin preparing the potion. It takes a good many hours to boil. Knowing the wolves and feeling how anxious they are, they will not delay for more than a day."

Weylyn! Weylyn!

Weylyn woke in a cold sweat, sitting straight up in bed. Panting, he looked around the room reminding himself where he was and why. His night terror scared him more than he admitted. Watching Eithne in pain and not being able to reach her... He worried it was a vision, not a dream. Standing, he found his trousers and pulled them on. Walking over to the door leading to the balcony, he opened it and allowed the cooler air to wash over his heated skin. Needing to know his mate was well, he phased and searched for Blane. He found him rushing around the keep, barking orders to the others. Blane's body was buzzing. Something was wrong.

Blane?

The nomadic wolf froze but turned his consciousness to Weylyn.

Weylyn.

What is wrong? What has happened? When Blane did not answer, the fear in the pit of his stomach grew. *Eithne.*

She was attacked by a dark force. Bowdyn found her but

the pup is coming and the druids fear...

Weylyn's body tingled with heightened emotions. *Where is she?* He demanded.

With her sisters and Bowdyn is helping keep the wards up around the keep in case there is another attack.

I must see her. Please, Blane.

Blane took a moment but then nodded and called for another wolf to take over. Weylyn did not speak as he waited for Blane to reach the room where Eithne's cries of pain were heard. When Blane opened the door, Weylyn nearly collapsed from fear. His mate was pale as death and a fever raged within her, sweat poured from her brow as she moved her head back and forth crying out and muttering something about a dark druid. Isla and Labhaoise soothed her forehead and lay strips of cloth over her heated skin.

"Weylyn," she moaned. "Weylyn. Where are you?"

"I am here," Weylyn cried.

Easy, my friend, donnae give her false hope. Blane tried to calm him. *She is fighting the effects of the poison.*

What poison?

Someone created a trap. She went for water and there was a dark power hidden in the larder. When she opened it, it attacked her. The poison caused her to see things that were nae there.

Dear gods, I need her ken I am here. Please Blane, go to her. Hold her for me. I beg you.

He felt Blane's indecision. Finally, he agreed and with a look at his mate, Odara tending the fire and boiling a tisane, he walked over to Eithne.

"Blane?" Isla questioned. He looked at her and she nodded. "Weylyn, she needs you."

"I am here," Blane said using Weylyn's words. "Eithne, my love." He sat on the bed and took her in his arms. "I am here.

Please my love. Fight for me."

"Weylyn, Weylyn," Eithne moaned. "Need you. Darkness. Help me."

"What do you need, my love? Please tell me." Weylyn sounded so desperate even to his ears.

"Dagda," she groaned. "Help. Weylyn. Please."

Her words made no sense, but it angered Weylyn. Could Dagda have been the one to set the trap? Only the darkest druids would know how to attack someone like that.

Please keep her safe, Blane. Stay with her.

Where are you going?

To get answers.

Weylyn phased back to his human form and threw open the main door to his bedroom. Stalking down the hall to his son's room, he did not knock before he barged in. Aedan was out of the bed in a moment, half-phased, with his dirk in his hand, steady and read to fight.

"Da'?" He questioned when he saw him. Phasing back to his human form, he continued. "Gods above, donnae do that. I could have hurt you..." then, seeing his father's face, he knew something was not right. "What is wrong?"

"Where is the dagger?" Weylyn demanded.

Aedan's brow furrowed. "Why do you need it?"

"Where is it, Aedan?" Weylyn bellowed. Never having raised his voice to his son before, Aedan was immediately concerned.

"What is going on, da'?"

"So help me boy you tell me where that dagger is, or I swear I will give you a challenge you will nae be able to recover from."

Aedan saw the fear in his father's eyes. "Eithne," he stated. "What has happened? Is she hurt?"

"Where is it?" Weylyn shouted.

"What is going on here?" Tristan stumbled into the room; his eyes puffy with sleep.

"Stay out of this, Alpha," Weylyn did not turn to him but kept his eyes fixed on Aedan.

"Weylyn?" Tristan asked surprised. "What?"

"I said this does nae concern you, Pup now get out of my way." Weylyn turned to him, his yellow eyes caught the dagger resting on the desk beside the fireplace.

Tristan locked eyes with Aedan. When Weylyn turned back to the door, Lucien's Dagger in hand, Tristan blocked the exit.

"What is going on?" Tristan asked, his voice calm trying to understand Weylyn's sudden change.

"Get out of my way," Weylyn's low tone commanded.

"No' until you tell me what is going on."

"So help me, Tristan you get out of my way now, or Dagda will no' be the only one I use this dagger on."

"Dagda?" Tristan and Aedan asked together.

"Weylyn, my friend," Tristan went on. "Whatever it is, we will figure this out together, all of us. What has happened?" Weylyn's eyes were on fire. Tristan mustered all the Alpha Power he could into his next words. "Tell me what is going on, Weylyn. And tell me now."

Weylyn's body shook as he felt the power in his alpha's voice. "Dagda laid a trap and Eithne stumbled upon it. She is dying."

"What?" both the males said together.

"I need to ken what he did so I can tell Isla and Labhaoise and they can save her. Get out of my way."

Weylyn pushed passed Tristan and froze when he was in the hallway. "Da'?" Aedan rushed out when he realized

Weylyn was not moving. Dagda and Lucien stood at the end of the hallway, staring at Weylyn, having frozen him in place much like Dagda did to Tristan on the way there.

"Release him," Tristan demanded.

"Not until he calms down." Dagda's eyes turned to the dagger in Weylyn's hand. "What is this nonsense of me setting a trap?"

"We ken no'," Aedan replied. "Da' was no' making much sense."

"So I gathered," Lucien stated. "Dagda," he motioned for his son to move toward Weylyn.

"Donnae harm him," Tristan challenged.

"I will not," Dagda said. "But talking to a wolf so out of control of his emotions wastes time. 'Tis much easier to do this." Dagda raised his hands to Weylyn's head and closed his eyes. Weylyn stayed frozen as Dagda searched his memories. "It is a jumble. But it appears as though his mate was attacked. I need more information. He knows very little."

Dagda looked at Tristan and Aedan. Aedan nodded to his alpha and Tristan half-phased. Seeking out Blane's consciousness. He still held Eithne.

Blane, do you ken what happened? Tristan asked.

Alpha, thank the gods. Only what Bowdyn told me. Blane answered.

Where is Bowdyn?

Commanding the men, Blane explained.

I must speak with him.

And Eithne? Weylyn asked me no' to leave her.

It is more important we figure out what happened to her.

Aye, Blane stood and without another word, went in search of Bowdyn. Tristan saw the tall, lean druid commanding the males on the battlements to be prepared for another attack. Blane called out of him and Bowdyn came running down the stairs.

"Has something changed with Eithne? Is she well?"

"My alpha needs to ken what happened. We are connected. Speak to me as you would him."

Bowdyn nodded and bowed slightly. "Alpha, I ken little, but I will tell you what I saw." Tristan allowed Dagda to read his mind as Bowdyn explained what happened and as soon as the dark druid saw the magic and felt what Bowdyn felt, he tensed. Taking a step back from Tristan, Dagda turned to his father, their eyes met, and Lucien raised his chin slightly. They knew what was going on. Weylyn still stood frozen, pain entering his eyes and a single tear slid down his cheek. Aedan went over to his father and placed a hand on his shoulder so he could feel his son's comfort.

"Release my father, Druid. He is worried for his mate."

"He has the dagger, I do not trust him with it," Dagda replied.

Aedan walked around to stand in front of his father. He maneuvered the dagger to be level with his chest. "Da', you continue, and you will hurt me. I beg you, let Dagda and Lucien help us. They clearly did nae do this. Eithne needs you. Please Da', let the dagger go."

Weylyn's eyes pleaded with his son as another tear slid down his cheek. Aedan wiped it away. "Please da', donnae make a liar out of me. Calm and let them help us. Look down if you agree." Seeing Weylyn finally look down, Aedan nodded to Lucien. With a flick of his wrist, Lucien released Weylyn. Immediately Weylyn lowered the dagger from Aedan's chest and allowed Tristan to take it from him. Weylyn shook with fear and unshed tears. His mate was dying, and he could not be there. History was repeating. All Weylyn could see when he looked at his son was Brietta. She died in his arms years ago. Was he doomed to have it repeat, but to where he could not even hold

Eithne once more? Tears ran unchecked down his face. Aedan ushered him into his room and shut the door allowing Tristan to handle the two dark druids. They walked to the balcony and Aedan turned his father toward him.

"'Tis all right."

Weylyn fell into his son and he screamed into his shoulder. Aedan felt every wrack of sobs from his father as surely as if they were his own. He felt his father's heart break and the pain was overwhelming.

"She is still alive," Aedan tried to encourage.

"For how long?" Weylyn wailed.

"Let Dagda and Lucien help. They recognized the magic. Let them help. Eithne will be well. I ken it, Da'. She is strong."

"I should never have left her."

"I ken you think that, but she is well. Focus on that."

Weylyn cupped his son's jaw, staring into his eyes.

"She is nae mum, da'. She is nae going to leave you."

Weylyn shook his head. "You donnae ken that."

"Aye, I do. There is a cure. We just have to find it."

Aedan pulled Weylyn in and embraced him tightly. "I ken the fear and pain you are enduring, but take heart in the truth, you have many others with you who will always fight for you. Who love you. You mean so much to so many. We will all fight for you. Always and forever. I swear it."

Chapter Eight

Tristan let Aedan take Weylyn into the room and comfort him, but his heart ached for his dearest friend, knowing what he went through with Brietta. He turned to Dagda and Lucien.

"You both understand the pain my Beta is going through. I can see it in your eyes. He already lost a mate, Aedan's mother was killed and died in his arms. Please, I beg of you, do what you can to save Eithne. I will owe you a debt if you do. You may collect anytime, for any reason, nae questions asked. Please. Save my Beta's mate."

"The power is a strong one. It is Bióg's," Lucien stated.

"The same who attacked us on our way here?" Tristan

asked.

"The same," Dagda agreed. "She must have assisted this Liam Arc'hantael. It would not surprise me if she did not know the pack had aligned with me."

"Biróg is a dark Fae and a druidess. She was my wife's dearest friend's great-grandmother. Centuries ago, when Myrna introduced her friend to her grove, Myrna's father, the high priest, fell in love with the lass. They married and had a daughter, Deena, the most powerful of all druidesses, because she was part Fae. Fae power descends from mother to daughter."

"Fae?"

"*Tuatha Dé Danann*, the fairy folk of Erin and Alba. Very powerful creatures. Those who attacked you on the road here. The Sprites are the playful offspring, but not all are playful," Dagda explained.

"*Those* were playful?" Tristan demanded, remembering the evil entity that tried to seduce him.

"There has been a war between realms for many centuries. Biróg demanded my help with something but I refused. She turned her attention to my children."

"Delia and I have eluded her for years," Dagda replied. "My brother Flynn, however, was not so fortunate. Biróg told him... details of his origin and he grew angry. He agreed to help her in whatever manner she needed. Even seduced and convinced my betrothed, I was evil. Geileis stole the dagger and gave it to Flynn. He was going to kill my family."

"But what is her connection with us? We donnae live on this isle, and we have nothing to do with the Fae world," Tristan said.

"In a way you. Deena was married to Alasdair, the first of your kind. So you each have a little Fae blood, but since you are all male, the power is dormant. Biróg seeks out those most powerful... Caylean must have been a beacon of light for her and when he left Dagda's grove, she must have followed him to Alba."

"Did he ever tell you he kenned this… creature?" Tristan asked.

"Nay," Dagda replied. "But she is cunning, she could have been hiding in plain sight. She could have tricked him or even…"

"Even what, lad?" his father questioned.

"She could have poisoned his ear as he slept…" Dagda said. "She is in my grove."

"Who?" Tristan asked.

"I do not know, but how else?" Dagda demanded.

"We must get you back to your grove with all haste. If what you believe is true, Dagda, she may have already corrupted Caylean beyond repair," Lucien stated.

Aedan and Weylyn walked out of the room and looked from one to the other.

"What did we miss?" Aedan asked.

"I will tell them, Dagda, you go and prepare what must be prepared." Tristan offered.

"Myrna needs but a small amount of blood from the one closest to Caylean, his blood kin," Lucien replied. His eyes turning to Aedan. "For the spell to locate him."

Without hesitation, Aedan offered his wrist to Dagda. With a twist of his wrist, a vial appeared in Dagda's hand and he took his small eating knife from his side sheath, approaching Aedan. Without a flinch, Aedan allowed him to cut his wrist and pour the blood into the small container. Once there was enough, Aedan accepted Lucien's help and he healed the wound.

"My mate?" Weylyn's voice cracked when the two druids turned to leave.

"We must break Biróg's hold on Caylean and only then will her powers weaken," Dagda replied. "But until then, I will give your druids a spell to help her. She will be well, Weylyn. I promise you. I ken what it is like to lose someone you love, and I will never allow another to go through that. Especially not my own kin. Do not fear for your mate, my friend. I need you here, now, ready to face the challenges before you. Eithne will be well."

Weylyn nodded and watched the two druids disappear around the corner. Turning to Tristan, their alpha explained what was discussed.

Lucien slammed the door to his master room and paced. Myrna looked up from the fire and potion boiling, over the roaring flames.

"What has happened?" she asked, seeing the look in his eye.

"I swear Biróg has hurt my kin for the last time," he growled.

"Lucien, talk to me," Myrna rushed over to him. "Please, my love."

Lucien paused a moment then turned to his wife. "She has cast darkness over Weylyn's mate."

"Oh nay," Myrna breathed. "But I am sure she will be well. From what he said at dinner, she is not the usual Druid—"

"She is carrying a pup."

Myrna's eyes grew wide and her hand flew to her mouth. "Gods' nay."

"Aye, I tried to tell Weylyn not to fear but…"

"Dearest, it is not your fault. None of it."

"It is," he countered and paced to the window. "If I had not dismissed her, if I had done what she asked, she would never have come after my family. Now, Weylyn may lose his soulmate and child."

"You believe that is her terms? To take his child? The pup is hardly strong in the ways of a druid. Eithne is not a high priestess. Now Giorsal's and Caylean's child, perhaps."

"Weylyn is the heartbeat of the group. If he hurts, they all do, and they will all want revenge."

"What did you sense? Is she going to be all right?"

"It is affecting her differently, because…" he paused. "I cannot say yet, we must find her and break her hold on Caylean. Only then will her spell break on Eithne."

"There must be something we can do."

"There is, but not from here."

"Then send me, Lucien. Send me to her. Let me help."

Lucien looked at his mate remembering the day a millennium ago when she agreed to be his and the utter sickness and hopelessness he felt when she was taken from him.

"With you there, you will be able to slow the progress of the spell. It is perhaps the best way. I will go with Dag and the wolves and finish this once and for all."

"I know you will," she said. "If anyone can, it is you, my love. Be careful."

He kissed his wife but before they could do more, he pulled back and saw the passion in her eyes fade to determination.

"Take at least two others with you. At night when the moon is high, I will come to you. Tell me what is going on. Together we will make the way safe for our family."

"I will expect you when the moon is high. Let me gather the things I need. You will need to finish the potion for the locator spell. Do you have the blood?"

Lucien produced the vial of blood from beneath his robes. "Pray this works. Though I am fairly certain I know where he is."

"As do I. Do you believe he is as strong as Jeeran?" She asked.

"I do, but unlike Jeeran, Caylean let his mate go. He does not have her to keep him grounded."

"But you remember there was a darkness in Jeeran. He had too much of my father in him," she said.

"True, but he had his family. The only time his darkness took over was when Alasdair passed. Though he was grown with grown children of his own, any man who loses their father is permitted to embrace the darkness for a time especially when they were as close as those two were."

"Agreed. But you remember what happened..."

"I do, I pray Caylean is still in control. It will be much more difficult to reason with his wolf self," Lucien said.

"If anyone can, it would be you. Now, let us finish preparing the spell. I will call Dagda in. You know how drained you get when you perform this," Myrna passed a hand over her husband's eyes.

"It is draining," Lucien agreed. "Call our son. I will finish the potion and prepare."

As Myrna left the room, Lucien headed to the fire and stirred in the blood. Even though he had been a druid for longer than he cared to remember, originally, he was a human, a Highlander and every time he or his wife did a potion spell his stomach and mind rebelled. A locator spell was something only certain druids were willing to perform. It was difficult but for him, being part wolf, his self-preservation would take over and fight the affects.

Whenever he performed the ritual, he saw through his wolf eyes and sometimes it was difficult for the animal to explain what he saw. Dagda usually read his mind, so he saw the same things and was able to interpret what was revealed.

The potion ready, Lucien pulled it off the fire and prepared his body for the pain.

Chapter Nine

Dagda knocked on his parent's bedroom door and walked in, seeing his father staring down into the fire. A moment's hesitation flooded his system, seeing his father look so defeated. Every time he asked Lucien to do the spell, it took a toll on him.

"Da'?" He questioned. Lucien looked up and smiled slightly. "Are you well?"

"Aye, just thinking."

"Preparing?"

"I hear the regret in your voice, lad. I am well. Do not think I am not. But I am glad you are here. Let us get this over with." Leaning forward, Lucien took the cup and ladle from the side table.

Filling it with the potion, Lucien took a deep breath, sat back, and let his son kneel beside the chair. Bringing the foul-smelling potion to his lips, he swallowed down the bile that rose in his throat, tipped the cup back, and drank it down.

Weylyn felt like he was dying, the pain was intense. Seeing his mate through Blane's eyes, Eithne lay still, for the first time that day. She rested. He watched her chest rise and fall, focusing on the next breath.

Live for me, my love. Please.

She will be well, Weylyn. I promise, Blane said.

You cannae promise that.

The door opened and his son's scent filled his nostrils.

"Have you slept?" Aedan asked, walking over to his father.

Weylyn shook his head. "I cannae. No' until I ken she is well."

"You will be of nae use to us if you donnae get your rest."

He is right, Weylyn. Eithne rests, 'tis your time, Blane said.

"Will you stay phased, Aedan?" Weylyn begged. "If anything happens..."

"I will remain vigilant, da'. I promise," Aedan swore. "Rest." Aedan half-phased, sought Blane's conscious, and connected with him. Nodding once at Weylyn, he watched his father phase back to his human form and walk dejectedly to the bed.

Lying down, Weylyn took a deep heavy breath, closed his eyes and fell into a restless sleep.

Tell me what you donnae want to tell him, Aedan said to Blane.

She is nae doing well. Isla worries for the pup. The magic is dark. I overheard the druids speaking in hushed tones. They worry of the effect on the pup. I understand, under normal circumstance, the person under the spell can work through the affects but with the pup... they donnae ken how it will be affected. And it is affecting her differently.

Could the pup die?

Aye and take her with it.

That is nae possible.

They say it could be.

Gods nay. Please stay with her.

I will nae leave her.

Thank you, my friend. I am here if you need me. Aedan silenced the connection between them, poured a cup of whisky, and sat by the fire.

"What do you see?" Dagda questioned his father.

Lucien writhed on the chair; his thoughts scattered. Dagda was unable to focus on what was being shown.

"Water, falls," Lucien gritted out. "Green."

"Narrow it down," Dagda ordered.

"I cannae, he is strong. He is blocking me."

"What do you feel?"

"Empty. There is nothing. No pain, no love, no life. But a dizzying power unlike any I have ever felt."

"Talk to him," Dagda urged.

"He will nae let me," Lucien answered.

"Let me talk to him then," Dagda offered.

"He will not," just then Lucien roared, threw his head back and howled. When he opened his eyes, they were black with yellow pupils.

"You think you can best me?" A voice foreign to his father's spoke. "You think you can find me? You cannae save your own!"

"Caylean?" Dagda asked.

"Caylean is nae here. Only me. You cannae best me. Stop trying!"

"I swear to you, Caylean, we will save you."

"Save him? He is fine. It is what he wants. He is weak but I am strong. He is mine! You cannae do anything."

"We will find you. You will be with Giorsal again."

Lucien roared, his body pitched forward, and Dagda ducked just as Lucien vomited the potion.

All was quiet as Lucien went slack in the chair.

"Da'?" Dagda asked.

"I am well," his voice was strained but back to his usual tone. "I have never felt power like that. He was too strong, even for me."

"How?"

"I believe he has allowed his wolf to take over. But he is still there. When you said Giorsal, I felt his despair and pain. He is still there."

"Did you see anything? Do you know where he is?"

"Aye. I did see something."

Chapter Ten

Aedan rushed to the door when he heard the frantic knocks. Opening it, Tristan, Dagda, and Lucien burst in. Weylyn woke with a start and looked over.

"We need to leave. Now," Dagda said.

"What? Why?" Aedan demanded.

"We found Caylean. We know where he is. But..."

"But?" Weylyn pressed standing and walking over to his son.

Dagda looked at his father and Lucien nodded.

"My father performed the locator spell. It looks as if

Caylean has returned to my grove, but it also seems his human side has retreated to the far corners of his mind. His wolf has taken over," Dagda explained.

"What does that mean?" Weylyn asked.

"We are unsure," Dagda admitted. "The only time that has happened, wolves go mad. Caylean is still phased as a human, but the wolf has taken over. I fear if we do not go and confront him quickly, he may be lost forever. Biróg has a strong hold on him but his own blood is working against him."

"What do you mean?" Aedan demanded.

"He is your son, conceived just after your first phase. Your wolf essence was strong, undiluted which has never happened since wolves usually phase far too early in life. Isla's child would be strong anyway as she is high priestess. But most importantly, he has Alpha blood in him. Not only Alpha blood but Marrock's line, my wife's father's blood. He is the strongest creature I have ever encountered," Lucien explained.

"Perhaps it is time I also mention he was conceived under the Hunter's Moon..." Aedan offered.

Lucien looked at him then rolled his eyes skyward. "Why do I even bother asking questions when you do not tell me the whole truth?" He muttered. "'Tis no wonder the lad is powerful. It would have helped knowing this earlier."

"Can he be reasoned with?" Weylyn asked.

"Unless we can reach his human side, no. I do not believe he can. And being immortal, he cannot be killed either. If he allows Biróg's influence, his Reign of Terror would be stronger than Marrock's and would last for eternity."

"You said his wolf took over, but he is still human, so we play to the human side," Tristan offered.

"He is stronger than any I have ever sensed," Lucien said. "This is not going to be easy."

"He is my son," Aedan stated. "I will do everything in my

power to help him and take care of him. I will get him back to his mate."

Tristan growled softly. "I still donnae like how he left my daughter, but I understand his need to protect those he loves... I will nae hold it against him. He is a good lad."

"I thank you, my friend," Aedan replied. "Now, let us go. The sooner we can find him, the sooner this witch's hold on Eithne will be released."

Sensing his father's fear, Aedan turned to him, placed a hand on his shoulder, and squeezed. "Nae change. She still rests."

Weylyn nodded but the fear did not leave his eyes.

"One more thing," Lucien said. "I need a vial of Weylyn's blood."

"What for?" Aedan asked.

"The spell to help his mate requires the blood of the one who loves her the most," he explained.

"I have seen this spell before," Weylyn said. "Mabh was used to save Marrock many years ago, before you were born, Tristan."

"Aye," Lucien replied. "It is a simple spell, but it will help her."

"Then do it," Weylyn stated. "Do whatever it takes."

Lucien produced a vial and took what he needed. They gathered their things as Lucien took the vial to Myrna and soon, they left the keep through the hidden cave entrance and down the mountain.

Chapter Eleven

After a day of travel, Myrna looked up at the gates to the Wolf Village and waited as the sentry who stopped her, announced her to the lady of the keep. Tristan had given Myrna a pass phrase to say to the wolves and, most importantly, to his mate. Glancing beside her as her guard waited stoically, she was grateful, Lucien had sent him. The druid warrior had been in her husband's employ for centuries and they both counted him as a personal friend. He glanced over at her and nodded.

"All will be well, my lady," he said. Before she could answer, the gate opened and Myrna saw Tristan's human mate, Alexina. She stood tall, her blonde hair plaited, she wore no distinguishing marks apart from her mate's claim around her neck. The pendant bore Tristan's name in the language of the wolf.

"I am Alexina, mate to the Alpha. My guard tells me you have news of my husband and pack mates." Her voice was accented from her original home in the Highlands.

"I do, my lady," Myrna stated. "But your husband gave me a phrase to say to you so you would know it is he who sends me."

"And that phrase is?" Alexina asked.

"Remember the blossoming heather under the warmth of the sun, the day we named the First of Spring."

Alexina nodded, then looked over at her guard.

"Your husband is as cautious as mine, I see," Alexina said.

"When you have lived over a millennium, you become used to it," Myrna replied.

"I donnae think I will ever be used to it," Alexina smiled. "Come in. You are here to see to my sister?"

"Eithne is human?" Myrna asked concerned.

"Nay, but she is my sister nae less. We all claim each other as such."

"Ah, I see. Is there somewhere my guard can wait, so he is out of your way? He is a dear man but does hover."

The guard grunted. "My orders are to stay by your side, my lady."

"I am quite safe here," Myrna stated.

"Perhaps we could use you at the training circle. I am sure our young would enjoy meeting a great druid warrior," Alexina offered.

"Splendid idea. Harailt is a skilled warrior," Myrna replied.

Alexina's face went pale and a hush descended around

them. Her eyes never left the druid warrior.

"Are you well, my lady?" he asked when her gaze never faltered.

"Forgive me," Alexina replied. "You have the same name as my younger brother. He was murdered many years ago. The name took me off guard."

"I am sorry," he stated. "I also lost a beloved bother very young. If you point me in the direction of the training circle, I would be happy to assist your young."

"Thank you," Alexina indicated the location of training area and once he received Myrna's approval, he left.

"I am sorry for your loss," Myrna finally said.

"'Tis an old wound," Alexina admitted. "But it still hurts."

"Of course," Myrna replied. "It will always hurt but it is how we move forward that honors their memory." Alexina smiled slightly at her. "Now, enough worry and sadness. My husband has given me instructions on how to assist Eithne until they can break Biróg's hold on her. Please lead the way."

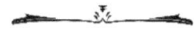

Caylean strode through the keep in Dagda's grove, coming to a stop at the entrance to his solar. Taking over Dagda's duties had been easier than he expected. Two druids challenged him, but they were swiftly dealt with and the others who created discourse and rumblings of a takeover were quickly thrown in prison. The others were either too cowardly or too intelligent to face him and agreed to name him their high priest.

He caught his eyes in the reflective surface of Dagda's crest hanging on the wall. The black with yellow pupils stared back at him. He felt something stirring in the back of his mind.

"Are you there?" he asked.

It took a moment but eventually he heard. *I am always here.*

The voice was his own, but the sound of defeat made him growl. "It has to be like this. I promised I would take care of us. This is what you wanted."

I never wanted murder.

"It was nae murder. They stood against us. They challenged us. Did you want that to go unanswered?"

There was no response. Without another thought, he opened the door to his solar seeing Kyriea, the first female he had experienced a couple years ago, waiting for him.

"What news?" She asked.

"Dagda tried to find me," he said.

"What did you do?" She asked pouring him a cup of whiskey.

He fell into his chair and gratefully accepted the drink. "I used it against him. He opened the door and I turned the tide." Kyriea slid down on his lap. The initial reaction of disgust was soon replaced by need. As soon as her lips latched onto his neck, he tried to push the thoughts away. But when her hand slipped down the front of his trousers, he pulled back. Her dark eyes questioned but when he looked away, she nodded.

"He is closer to the surface than you have told me."

He nodded. "He is still loyal to his mate and nothing I do will stop that."

"What about you? You first appeared when you saw her being attacked."

"She was my mate," he admitted. "But she will never be again."

"Do you still love her?"

His headache that came anytime his human side was close to overpowering him, roared to life. He groaned and lowered his head to his hand.

"He is close," he admitted. "I need to be alone." She stood

from his lap and poured another cup of whiskey. "Leave it," he stated. She did not hesitate and left the jug on the table by his elbow. When he was alone, he spoke low. "Why do you always stop it? We have needs."

I have nae needs.

"You cannae stop this for eternity."

I will stop you for now.

"You heard Kyriea. *She* would nae want us after everything. Why do you pine for her?"

When he did not answer for a time, the wolf sighed and poured a refill.

Wolves mate for life, he finally heard.

"We are nae wolf, we are hybrid," he stated and felt his human side retreat into the furthest reaches of his mind. His lust abated for a time, he paced to the desk and sat down.

He did miss his family, what little he could remember of them. He was not completely devoid of emotions but all he remembered was flashes and most of them were bloody and with looks of horror on their faces. Trying to concentrate to remember his father's face, or his mother's, he growled when he saw nothing but a bloody mess at his feet, then pain. His father had attacked him after he killed those in his pack. How could he be accepted by a family who attacked him with moon flower?

Growling in frustration, he downed his whiskey. Feeling the slight swimming of his mind, he reveled in it and, pouring another cup, he embraced the oblivion.

Chapter Twelve

Slowly Eithne's mind cleared enough to hear voices but she did not know where she was or why there were people around her as she slept.

"She should be coming around any moment," she heard a foreign voice say. "The potion worked better than I hoped."

Potion? She questioned. Moaning softly, the voices stopped.

"Eithne, love?" Isla's voice said, close to her. "Can you open your eyes?"

Eithne tried but they could only open to slits.

"Isla?" she croaked. Her throat hurt.

"Shh, try no' to talk," Isla said.

"My baby?" she asked, placing a protective hand over her stomach.

"He is still there, love," Labhaoise stated. "Drink this. You labored with him and darkness, but Myrna is here and she helped you. You may still feel the effects but 'tis better now, aye?"

She nodded and took a sip of tea. "When will he be born?" Eithne asked feeling the tightening of the skin around her stomach as she labored.

"The potion will slow the process," the foreign voice said. Eithne looked over and saw a light-haired woman standing by the fireplace. "We hope to slow it until my husband can break Biróg's hold. Once that happens, we will help your pup."

"What hold?" Eithne questioned.

"We will tell you all in a moment, but right now we must tell Weylyn you are well," Alexina stated. She leaned out the door and called for Blane. The nomadic wolf they claimed as a friend, walked in and smiled.

"Eithne," he breathed. "Thank the gods. I have felt Weylyn's despair. He will be most pleased to see you awake."

"Please, phase, Blane," she agreed as Labhaoise helped her sit up. "Let me tell my mate I am well."

Blane nodded and half-phased.

The pack ran as wolves through the forests and glens of Erin. Dagda's grove was south-east on the other side of the isle. They did not stop, eager to reach the shore.

Weylyn ran between Tristan and Lucien. Aedan ran on the other side of Tristan beside Dagda. None of them said anything, focused on crossing the human areas quickly.

Suddenly, Blane's conscious entered their minds.

Weylyn!

Weylyn froze midstride at the urgency he heard in Blane's voice.

Dear gods, nay. Was all he could say.

Nay, my friend! Be at ease. She is well. Lucien's mate's potion worked for the time being. Look! Blane looked down at Eithne and Weylyn groaned.

Oh, my love, thank the gods! Are you well?

Blane spoke the words as Weylyn thought them.

"I am, my love. Our pup is coming soon, but I feel better. I am sorry for scaring you. Myrna says if you can break someone's hold then she will be able to assist me with the delivery," Eithne explained.

"And it will be without complication," Myrna spoke. "Do not fear, Weylyn. Find Caylean and break Biróg's curse."

We will. I swear it. I love you, Eithne. I will return soon.

"I will be waiting. I love you, Weylyn. Promise me you will be safe."

I swear it. Tell our pups I love them, and we will be home very soon.

When Eithne promised she would tell their sons and said she loved him once more, he turned his mind to Blane.

I thank you, my friend. For truly I would nae have been able to leave her without your help and connection.

'Tis my pleasure, Weylyn. Now go and concentrate on what is needed. My alpha, is there anything I need to ken or do? Blane asked Tristan.

Nay, Tristan answered. *I have left the pack in good hands. Thank you, Blane. If you need us, call for us.*

I will, Alpha. Thank you. Blane broke the connection and phased back to human form.

Aedan looked over at his father and, if a wolf could smile, he would have but with a nod, he praised the gods for their mercy.

They arrived at the outskirts of Dagda's lands. When the dark druid slowed, the rest of them went silent allowing him to sense. His father growled softly, clearly communicating with his son. But since they were not from the same pack, they could not hear what Lucien was saying and waited.

Dagda phased back to human form and untied the pouch tied around his ankle, pulling out his trousers. Weylyn, Aedan and Tristan did the same. Lucien stayed in wolf form.

"My father is going to stay guard. We must go. I sense a darkness here. Let me do the talking, if however, I feel he would respond better to you I will turn to you and nod," Dagda explained.

"This is your land, Druid," Tristan began. "We follow you."

Dagda raised his brows, clearly not expecting that from Tristan. "Do any of you have special names for him?" Dagda asked.

"I do," Weylyn spoke.

"Good, when I look at you, call him that. It will tell me how strong Biróg's hold is on him."

They nodded. With one final look at his father, Dagda straightened to his full height and walked toward the gate.

Chapter Thirteen

Caylean looked sharply over at Kyriea. "He is here," he said.

"I sense it too," she replied. "But remember, you are Alpha now. You are our leader. He means nothing... Is *he* contained?" Caylean nodded. "Good. He will use *her* against you, you know."

"I ken," he answered. Then when she did not continue, he went on. "I am in control."

She framed his face and slipped down on his lap. "Good, then maybe after we can finally be together."

He swallowed down the bile that rose in his throat and forced his human side down as he grabbed Kyriea to him and kissed her deeply. Caylean roared in the back of his mind and forced memories of Giorsal to the front of his thoughts. When she first proclaimed she loved him, when they made love the first time, when he helped her with the bow and arrow, and when she cried for him even as his wolf tore away from her after being infected with the wolf's bane poison. Caylean's wolf self groaned and broke away from her.

"He is still there," she stated.

"I donnae ken if he will ever stop. I am sorry," he said.

"Nay, 'tis all right. Soon, once he has confronted his demons, he will vanish for good."

"I can only hope."

A knock at the keep's main door drew their attention. Caylean called for the person to enter. One of the druids bowed low. "Forgive this interruption, my lord. But we have visitors. They refuse to leave until they speak with you."

"Who are they?" Caylean asked, he had only sensed Dagda.

"I only know Dagda, my lord."

Caylean nodded. "I will receive them on the dais."

The druid bowed and left the room. Caylean turned to Kyriea. "Who could be with him?"

"I am not sure. Perhaps *she* sent an army after you."

"She would nae do that," he hissed.

"You defend her, still? You care for her."

"She was my mate for a time. I will nae have you disparaging her name or position."

Kyriea stood from his lap and sighed. "As you wish. But know he may use her against you. You know she would not want you after what you did. You are a monster in her eyes."

Caylean took a deep breath and nodded. "You are right. But let us go and show the Dark Druid that true power cannae be contained."

Dagda walked through the village keeping his face devoid of emotion when he saw the desolation. His people living in rags, the huts he had prided themselves on, destroyed. He stopped in his tracks when he saw the severed heads of two of his warriors on a spike beside the raised dais outside the keep. They were two of his best and two he had asked to stay behind to watch over the grove. And they were his personal friends. Hardening his features to give nothing away, he looked up at the dais.

Caylean sat on a throne. Kyriea beside him.

A spark of confusion entered Caylean's black eyes when he looked at Weylyn, Aedan, and Tristan. Dagda's brow furrowed. They reached the dais and stopped. No one spoke as Caylean stared into Dagda's eyes.

"Who do you bring with you, Dagda? An army? You are nae longer welcome here," Caylean's voice rang out but it was much deeper and rougher than they remembered. "I kenned you would try to bring an army to take it back, but as those two learned, you cannae defeat me." He motioned toward the two heads on the spike. "But truly, four of you? No' many. And an insult."

"Tell me," Dagda began. "Do you not recall who they are?"

Caylean shrugged. "It matters little."

Aedan caught Dagda's glance and stepped forward. "Son, I am your father, do you no' ken me?"

"I have nae father," Caylean stated as the memory of the bloody mess he always saw when he thought of a father, flashed across his mind.

Aedan lifted his hands. "I held you when you were but moments old. Nothing is dearer to me than you. You are of my blood. I trained you. I taught you how to shave the wood for arrows. I taught you how to fire a bow. I taught you how to be a warrior. I love you and will always be here for you."

Caylean's bored expression did not change. Dagda looked toward Weylyn.

"*Garmhac,*" Weylyn started. Caylean's body shook and he turned away from them. "*Garmhac,*" Weylyn tried again and again the same response. "'Tis me. I ken how you must feel but believe me, we want you home. We love you, *Garmhac.*" Every time Weylyn said the word *grandson* in Gaelic, Caylean shuddered.

"Nay! Gag him!" Caylean ordered and his alpha order affected all in his presence. Weylyn did not fight as one of the druids placed a gag around his mouth.

"Caylean," Tristan stepped forward. Caylean's eyes shot to him. "I ken you have nae memory of me or us but surely you must recall one."

"Namely?"

"Giorsal, your mate," Tristan stated.

Caylean shook and snarled. "That name is never to be mentioned."

"Giorsal. The one you left, alone and carrying your pup," Tristan declared.

Caylean's eyes widened and immediately changed to the brown of his human form. "What?"

"Giorsal carries a child, your child," Dagda went on. Caylean shook again and his eyes changed back to his wolf self.

"You lie! Giorsal cannae be with pup. I had the spell!"

"If you are as powerful as you say, you can read my mind. See what your mate went through. See her weeping on the floor. See how she cried when she told her father. After everything you did to her, she begged him to bring you back to her."

All went silent, then Caylean looked up at Kyriea who placed a hand on his shoulder. "I told you they would try to use her against you. You know she would never want you. Not after what you did. Why allow yourself the pain even for a moment?" She asked.

"'Tis you," Dagda said looking at Kyriea. Both of them looked at him. "You are Biróg."

"Is it you?" Weylyn demanded. Pulling off the gag, he yelled. "You cursed my mate!"

Biróg smirked and held out her hand as Weylyn ran toward her. Her palm outwardly extended to him, Weylyn stopped in his tracks. She then lifted her hand and Weylyn clutched at his throat as his body rose in the air.

"Release my father, Fae," Aedan shouted.

She laughed. "I am very glad to see my trap worked. You were so busy you did not even realize I had left long before you did, Dagda. And this mate of Weylyn's? She is with child, aye? Good. Let him suffer knowing her life is in my hands and the child will be mine. Do not think to stop me, Dagda. Your sister should have been mine, but your father forbade it and hid her from me. I will not let that happen again."

"Tell me, were you always Kyriea? Or did you inhabit her body?" Dagda asked.

"Do not worry, Dagda, you have only ever slept with Kyriea. I could not stomach the thought of you touching me. I merely inhabited her body a couple months ago. But make no mistake, Caylean is mine and together we will create the most powerful force on earth. The child of a Fae and a Hybrid. Eochaid will be dethroned and there is nothing you can do to stop it. I had hoped it would be Giorsal who had the spell attack her, but then the wolf's mate is just as good. No one is strong enough to stop me. Caylean cannot defeat his wolf and you are far too weak."

In that moment, Caylean's eyes turned brown and he leapt from the throne. Aedan threw him Lucien's Dagger. He caught it and rammed it through Biróg's back. The hag screeched.

"I am stronger than you both thought," Caylean spoke low into her ear. "I kenned they were coming so I bade my time. Be gone, hag. Neither of us wanted you." Caylean twisted the knife and Biróg let out a horrible scream. Weylyn fell to the ground from where she elevated him, unconscious from lack of air. Aedan immediately went to him.

Dark mist left Biróg's body and Dagda rushed forward. "Caylean, let go of the knife!" he yelled but it was too late. The smoke twisted around Caylean's arm and up to his mouth. Biróg vanished as Caylean gulped in the black mist. Weylyn roused and looked over as dark markings appeared all over Caylean's body and he grew as he phased to his hybrid wolf.

Dagda held Tristan back as he tried to rush to his son by marriage. Everything was silent. Caylean still stood, but on his wolf legs, his eyes closed.

"Caylean?" Dagda questioned softly.

It took a moment, but the creature's eyes popped open and they glowed red with the fiery orbs of a Fae. The creature took a deep breath and let it out with a satisfied sigh. "Dagda," he said, and the voice echoed as if it was two entities combined. But the voice was not menacing. "The power..." he smiled. "'Tis... intoxicating."

"Caylean, give it up. It is not what you want," Dagda cautioned.

"But I can have anything I want."

"Nay, you cannot. Believe me, lad. It will be too strong for you. You will lose more than you desire. Trust me. I care for you. This is not what you want."

His eyes narrowed and his face darkened. "You want it for yourself," Caylean challenged.

"You know that is not true," Dagda replied sternly. "But it will be too strong for you."

"I am stronger than you think," he answered.

"Caylean, please listen to him, son," Aedan pleaded, still kneeling beside Weylyn, who was too weak to get up. "Think of Giorsal and your pup! Think of your mother and I."

"I am, father," he answered. "I am all powerful. I could protect you all. I will be a good father. Like you are."

"Like this?" Dagda questioned. "Look at yourself. You would not be able to hold your child."

"All that power could harm everyone you love!" Aedan shouted.

Caylean stopped a moment and looked at his father and grandfather, then without warning, let out a roar that was somewhere between a man's yell and a wolf's howl. He bent over and fell to his knees. Dagda and Tristan rushed to him as his momentum carried him over the dais.

Far too heavy and large for them, Caylean landed on top of both in a huff.

"What is happening to him?" Tristan demanded as they got up but Caylean began shaking violently.

"The power is too strong for him. It will kill him," Dagda explained.

Aedan and Weylyn came up to them. "What do we do?" Aedan questioned.

"I must draw it out of him like a poison. It is dangerous and I may need my father."

"I will go get him," Tristan said and took off running to the front gate.

"What do we do?" Weylyn asked.

"Help me by holding him," Dagda replied and Weylyn and Aedan took their positions on either side of Caylean. "Caylean, listen to me. If you ever want to see Giorsal again, you must release the power."

Caylean nodded rapidly. Dagda held Caylean's head between his hands and leaned over him. Hovering face to face,

Dagda sucked in a deep breath and the two beside him saw the black smoke leave Caylean's mouth and enter Dagda's. Dagda groaned and opened his eyes. They were red but dark smoke swirled behind them. Again, Dagda drew the black smoke into him. With each time, Caylean went more and more still.

Finally, Dagda took one more deep breath, and nothing came out of Caylean. Dagda fell to the side and groaned.

Caylean sat up and looked at his father and grandfather. "I thought I lost you, lad." Aedan embraced him, tightly.

"I am sorry, da'. I kenned you were coming, I had to stall my wolf and Kyriea. I kenned their plans and I had to do something. I never wanted to murder anyone."

"Why did you leave in the first place?" Weylyn questioned embracing him.

"How can you ask me that?" Caylean asked, his eyes travelling to his father's neck. "I nearly killed him."

"But you saved him too," Weylyn reminded him.

"It does nae excuse what I did."

"Caylean," Dagda finally spoke. "You could have come to me. You know I would have…" He could not continue as he collapsed onto his back in pain.

"What is wrong?" Caylean asked.

"It. Is. Too. Powerful," Dagda gasped out.

"Share with me or expel it!" Caylean ordered.

"I cannot," Dagda replied.

"Then let me take some back." Caylean took his mentor's hand and tried to draw the poison out but gasped when nothing happened.

"You have no powers for a time," Dagda finally said.

"What did you do?" Caylean felt tears in his eyes. "I could have saved you."

"Not without compromising you. I refuse to do that. You can still practice but..." Dagda cried out and writhed on the ground.

"Dagda!" Lucien's voice came from behind them. The dark druid ran to his son as Tristan hurried to Weylyn. "Share with me, son." Dagda writhed again and cried out. "Son, please."

Lucien took his hand and place a hand on his son's forehead. Dagda screamed once more, then his entire body went slack, and his eyes closed.

Silence spread.

Lucien gripped his son's hand. "Dagda?" he questioned. "Dag?" he shook his hand and then checked his breathing. "Dagda!" When there was no answer, Lucien shook his head. "Nay, nay, Dagda wake. Dagda, nay. Donnae do this. You cannae die. No' *my* son. Nay. Wake." He shook him but when Dagda's markings began to fade, Lucien cried out. "Nay! Dagda!"

Tristan placed a hand on his shoulder. "I am so sorry, my friend."

"Nay, I will nae allow him to die."

"Dear gods, forgive me!" Caylean cried. "He is my friend and I caused this."

"Nay, *Garmhac*," Weylyn stopped him. "He kenned what he was doing. I only wish there was a way to save him."

The druids of the grove surrounded them. Caylean looked up at them and stood. "I am to blame. I caused all of you pain. I will forever be ashamed that I did nae stop my wolf from hurting you and killing our brothers. Please. Do with me as you will."

The druids looked at each other then, a woman stepped forward. "We all have made mistakes, Caylean. We know who and what you are. You are our brother. You have been punished enough. There will be no more death."

The grove's chanter stepped forward to give Dagda the

last chant of the dead. But as soon as he started, Lucien stood and closed his fist. The chanter stopped speaking as if Lucien had taken his voice. "I will nae have my son taken from me. Any man or woman who tries, will face my wrath." His eyes turned yellow. "Need I remind you; I am a Highlander first and a Dark Druid second? I am unafraid of those who would try and take him." He turned to the wolves. "I am placing him in your hands. Protect him. Do not allow them to consecrate him."

"What are you going to do?" Tristan asked.

"He is going to save him," Weylyn replied. "Just as Dagda saved Labhaoise."

Without another word, Lucien walked through the doors of the Druid Village, up the small incline and to the passage tomb and megalith to the *otherworld.*

Chapter Fourteen

Tír na nÓg was beautiful but Lucien refused to look around. He had seen it all before. He needed to find his son.

"Dagda!" He shouted. "Dagda!"

"Lucien?" he heard a voice behind him say.

Lucien turned and came face to face with Oengus, god of Youth and Love and son of the *Tuatha Dé* king; Eochaid. His golden hair glistening in the sunlight and his light brown, almost golden eyes looked questioningly at Lucien.

"'Tis good to see you my friend," Oengus said. "What brings you to *Tír na*?"

"I need to find Dagda," he said.

Oengus looked at him for a moment, tilted his head to

one side and laughed. "My father is in counsel."

"Not *the* Dagda, *my* Dagda," he answered. "I have no reason to interrupt Eochaid."

"Surely your son is not here," Oengus said.

"He is, please we have little time until his earthly body succumbs."

"I am sorry, my friend. I have not seen him. When did he pass into our world?"

"Just moments ago," Lucien's voice cracked.

"Let us go, if anyone knows, it is my father or Donn."

Lucien nodded and walked with him to the Tara. Announcing themselves to the doorkeeper; Camall mac Riagail. Camall bowed to Oengus and went to announce them. Lucien waited what felt like years for the doorkeeper to return. Finally, Camall arrived and welcomed them inside.

"Oengus, what is the meaning of this interruption?" Eochaid Ollathair's booming voice called. Oengus bowed low to the king and All-Father, also known as *the Dagda*, meaning *good god*.

"Father, forgive this intrusion. Lucien MacConchor is here looking for his son."

"Lucien?" Donn, the god of the Dead and Lucien's personal friend and mentor questioned. "What are you doing here?"

"What does this have to do with us?" the king asked before Lucien could respond.

"Forgive me, my king," Donn began. "He is one of mine, a dark druid. I know him well."

"I, too, know this man and his son. They are true loyalist to you and our ways. His son is named after you, my king," the man beside him stated.

Eochaid looked at the young, handsome warrior beside

him.

"You vouch for him, Lug?" Eochaid asked.

"I do indeed, my king. *Fir Domnann* of their ilk are few," Lug stated.

"I do as well," Donn replied.

Eochaid motioned Lucien forward. "I know you..." he began. Lucien bowed low.

"I was one of the humans who fought with you, my king against the *Formorians* on the great plain of *Mag Tuired*," Lucien explained.

"Aye, aye now I remember," *the Dagda* said. "You fought well. I remember remarking to The Morrigan how well you fought. You are not from this isle though, they said you fought like a Scotsman."

"I was a Highlander when I was human. I am now and have been for over a millennium, a Dark Druid."

"A human turned Druid? That is a rare feat," the king said. "What brings you here?"

"My son, my king. He has passed," Lucien stated.

"I am sorry, but why have you come here?" Dagda asked.

"To beg you to take me instead. He was trying to save a man he considers a son."

Another man beside *the Dagda,* leaned over to him and spoke softly. Lucien strained to hear Belenus, the god of Healing.

"I felt your son enter my realm, Lucien," Donn said. *The Dagda* looked over at Donn the god of the Dead and nodded. "And I feel your agony as surely as if it was my own, even if you try to hide it. Both you and Dagda are my personal friends. And I count myself fortunate *the Dagda* has given me the power to give you your son back. Come with me and we will find him."

Lucien let out a breath and bowed. "May I beg one last request?"

"Namely?" Eochaid asked.

"Allow me to say goodbye to my mate?" Lucien begged.

Eochaid looked at Donn, questioningly. "Lucien, you misunderstand me. *Both* of you shall live," Donn replied. Lucien looked over at him, unsure if he heard correctly. "Our only request is for you and your son to continue serving us as you have for so many years."

"With honor," Lucien stated.

"There are few I would grant this to, Lucien," Eochaid stated. "But my son and two of my most trusted vouch for you. Tell your son he must always remember and to teach his sons the same."

"He has nae sons, my king," Lucien replied. "He is forbidden to take his mate."

Eochaid's brow furrowed. "By whom is he forbidden?"

"By the gods," he answered.

Eochaid looked around the room. "Who?"

"Me, my king," The Morrigan, goddess of War replied.

"But he has chosen a mate, has he not?" Anu, the Mother goddess asked.

"He has love for only one," Lucien replied. "But does as the gods decree. All in his grove are unable to mate."

"That is because he taught warriors and warriors cannot have a family and still be considered reliable," The Morrigan stated. "But I defer to the god of All and the Mother goddess. I release your son and his grove from that burden. He is free to claim his mate and have by her many children."

"I thank you," Lucien replied. "He will be glad to hear it. He has lived with his love for decades."

"Who killed your son, Lucien?" Donn asked.

His eyes drifted to Lug. "I am sorry, Lug. But it was Biróg."

"Though the woman saved me from my grandfather's wrath, I have no doubt she has changed. If you say it is she, then it is. With your permission, my king, I will confer with her and seek as to why."

"Granted, Lug," he answered.

"I believe I may be able to answer that for you," Lucien replied. "I refused something she requested."

"And that was?" Eochaid asked.

"To lie with her and father a child. I am loyal to my mate and refused. She has attacked my children and turned my wife's child against us," Lucien provided.

"Your wife's child?" Anu questioned.

"Aye, my queen, my wife was set upon by the Roman invaders. We know not which of them fathered him, but I always strived to treat him as mine. He was twisted by Biróg and it was used against him."

"Roman scum," The Morrigan spat. "But your wife is fine now?"

"Aye, I thank Belenus for his healing," Lucien said. "But I beg of you, we must hurry. My son's fleshly body…"

"Will be fine," Belenus stated. "I promise you. It is the least I can do for you after everything you have done for us."

"I thank you," Lucien breathed, his throat tight with emotion.

"Before you go back to your lands," Donn started. "There is someone I know will want to say hello to you." He stood and walked to him.

Lucien looked at him. "Who?"

Donn merely smiled and waved his hand offering him to go ahead of him.

Oengus followed but said nothing and as they reached the door of the castle, they all turned and bowed to the gods and goddesses. The king dismissed them. Oengus stayed in his father's realm when Donn and Lucien walked to the Underworld.

The lost souls cried out to Lucien, but he had handled it multiple times before and kept his eyes forward.

"I am sorry for your sorrow, my friend," Donn said. "To lose a child is terrible."

Lucien turned his eyes to the rocky island over which Donn reigned.

"Thanks to you and *the Dagda,* my son will survive," Lucien said.

"I wonder what he will ask for in return," Donn replied.

"What is your meaning?" Lucien turned to Donn, his red hair and dark eyes staring straight ahead. Donn was built like a warrior standing slightly taller than Lucien's impressive height.

"I mean *the Dagda* does little out of the kindness of his heart."

"He has asked me to continue practicing our ways," Lucien justified.

"Aye, but I do wonder if that is all," Donn shrugged. "Ignore me, my friend. I have worried recently. How long will we last? The human world is changing. Soon, they will have no need of us. Any of the gods. They have become far too dependent on themselves and look at themselves as gods. I claim not to be a god and there are greater gods than me. Soon, we will be obsolete. The things of legend and, gods forbid, myth. But we are here. And we will always be here. Man needs a savior, maybe they already have one, maybe one is to come but however this world turns out, know one thing, the Fae will always exist. And we are always watching. Even when we are ignored, forgotten, dishonored, we still are here. Even we have a savior, though we don't deserve him, but he is always there. Always. You do not know him, there are many who do not, but he gives such peace, such comfort. I have never seen the like. Believe me, Lucien, he is indescribable, and he will save any who come to him. If they just believe."

"Of whom do you speak?"

"When you know him, you will know. We are nothing compared to his greatness. Many will be persecuted; many will die but his peace is everlasting."

"I would like to know that peace."

"I will send him your way," Donn said with a wink. "Now let us find your son. For indeed, He lost a son once. Only to have him again. He knows of your pain. He is merciful. Come, my friend." They entered the realm of the dead. "There is no need to call for Dagda. Think of him in your heart. He will appear," Donn said.

Lucien closed his eyes, believing his son would find a way to him. His memories of Dagda started when his wife labored to bring forth the life within her. Holding him in his arms for the first time, raising him as a young boy. Playing and training with him. Teaching him the ways of being a druid. His first phase into a wolf. The first time he came to Lucien in tears because his favorite pet died. The first time he said the gods spoke to him, the time he was told to start his own grove. The time Lucien was with him and he met Agora, the daughter of a local farmer and his druidess wife. The first time his son said he was in love. His first mark from when he dabbled in the dark arts. The times they sat together with a cup of mead or whiskey, speaking of everything on their minds or saying nothing at all. And the last and most painful of all, his son dying in his arms.

Feeling a presence before him, Lucien opened his eyes and gazed at his son. Dagda was looking at him, his head tilted to one side, studying him.

"Hello, father," he finally said.

"Dag," he breathed. "I have come to bring you home."

"But I am home."

"Aye, as I always wished but this is not your fleshly

home. Do you remember that place?"

Dagda studied him for a moment. "Aye," he finally said. "There are flowers and sunshine. Did I like apples?"

"Aye, you did," Lucien said with a smile.

"What is an apple?" The first day or so in the Underworld, all souls forgot who and what they were, but it soon ends and they begin to remember.

"Come back with me and I will show you," Lucien offered his hand. His son reached forward about to accept but pulled back.

"I cannot."

"You can," Donn said from beside him. "You need no permission, but you have it. Go, Dagda with the full love and support of my people."

Dagda looked at Donn then back at his father. "But it is nice here."

"'Tis," Lucien agreed. "But your mother and I are not ready to let you go. And Agora, she loves you. You have a chance to be with her. Do you want to?"

"Agora," he started nodding slowly. "I love her."

"Aye, and you can be with her, now," Lucien stated. "Just come with me. Please."

Dagda nodded and accepted his father's hand. The moment their hands connected, Dagda cried out, then looked back at his father.

"Da'?" he questioned. "What is happening?"

"You are well, son," he said. "We must go."

"Before you go, Uncle," he heard behind him.

Lucien smiled lightly and turned. "Alasdair, Fillion, Jeeran, Deena," he said. His nephews and Deena stood behind him. "Dear gods it is good to see you."

"Aye, Uncle," Fillion stated. "We have missed you."

"And I you," he replied.

Deena went up to him and embraced him. "Please tell my sister I love her, and I am here if she would like to speak to me."

"I will, lass," he answered.

"We ken you must go, Uncle," Alasdair said. "But we had to see you. Be sure to speak to us, aye? We can hear."

"I will," he answered. "I love you my lads."

"We love you," they said.

"But go. We will see you again but not for many many years. Be well, Uncle, Cousin," Alasdair looked from Lucien to Dagda.

"Come now, you must go. Remember my warning, my friend," Donn said. "I will keep you updated with any news."

"My thanks," Lucien said, then with a final look at his nephews and Deena, he pulled Dagda's spirit into him and woke in the megalith. Feeling his son's spirit within him, Lucien left the passage tomb and found the entrance to Dagda's grove. The wolves were still around his son's body and, with a nod of thanks, Lucien leaned over him, tilted Dagda's head back and open his mouth. Hovering over his son, he breathed life into him. The spark of Dagda's lifeforce passed from Lucien and Dagda woke with a gasp.

Chapter Fifteen

Dagda gasped awake and caught his father's gaze beside him. "Dag?" Lucien asked framing his son's face.

"Aye," he answered. Then, looking at the wolves around them, he continued. "What happened?"

"Your markings..." Caylean said. "They are gone."

Lucien and Dagda looked at his arms and Dagda blinked; his right eye had healed as well.

"I still have all memory of the spells, but I have no markings," Dagda questioned.

"You have been reborn," Lucien replied. "And you are free."

"I do not remember what happened, but I know you saved me. Thank you, da'." Dagda grasped his father's shoulder and embraced him.

"The true thanks goes to the gods," Lucien revealed. "They allowed you to come back."

"I feel... different."

"You are not confined any longer. We must thank the gods and then journey back to the Wolf Village."

Tristan turned his ear to something the rest of them could not hear, then smiled and looked at Weylyn.

"I believe someone wants you to phase," he said. Weylyn looked at his alpha, a mixture of fear and trepidation in his eyes. Finally, he phased and immediately Blane's consciousness entered his mind.

Weylyn! He cried; the smile evident from his tone. *All is well and Eithne has given birth to a beautiful lass.*

A lass? Weylyn questioned. All his children to that moment had been male. Secretly, he always wanted a little girl.

Aye, she is here. Weylyn looked down with Blane's eyes to see his mate holding a little bundle in her arms. The small face scrunched and asleep, but nothing had been more beautiful to him.

My mate?

Blane looked up at Eithne and she smiled.

"I am well, my love. Hurry home to hold our child."

I fly, my love. We will be home soon.

Weylyn took one more long look at his mate and daughter, then phased. His eyes and face alight with a happy smile.

"She is well, and I have a daughter!" Weylyn announced.

"Grand, 'tis glad I am, Da'," Aedan slapped his back.

"Many congratulations, Weylyn," Tristan said. "There is little joy like that of a daughter." His eyes turned to Caylean who looked away.

"I am sorry," he finally said. "I donnae deserve your forgiveness nor Giorsal's, but I swear to you, if you give me one more chance, I will never let you down again."

"Your wolf?" Tristan asked.

"He is gone," Caylean shrugged. "I donnae feel him."

"He may come back, like your powers, lad," Dagda said as his father helped him sit up. "But I very much doubt he will be the same as before." They were silent for a long moment, waiting for Tristan to render judgment.

An interminable time passed and finally, Tristan sighed.

"I promised my daughter to bring you home. As I see it, your fate is in her hands. Travel with us. But hear me, all of you, whatever my daughter chooses – to either recognize her mate or no' – I will follow. Nae one will change my decision."

"I expect nothing less, Alpha," Aedan replied. They all stood.

"Another thing," Tristan said and waited for Caylean to look at him. Once he did, Tristan pulled back and struck him. His fist collided with Caylean's jaw. Caylean, Aedan and Weylyn did not stop him. "That is for what you put my daughter through."

Caylean nodded not rubbing his jaw, allowing the pain to wash over him. "I am sorry," Caylean spoke low. "I thought I was protecting her and then Biróg told me lies and I retreated. My wolf self could nae remember my life before. All he remembered, was doing something hideous and leaving. Something nae one could ever forgive."

"You are forgiven, son," Aedan replied. "Come home with us now and let us prove it."

Caylean looked from one to the other of them and finally nodded.

"Thank you," he said.

"Journey with us, Dagda, Lucien," Tristan offered.

"We thank you as our mates are across the see in Alba. But I am sorry you will miss the sun rise on the river. 'Tis beautiful."

"No' as beautiful as my daughter's face," Weylyn said.

"Aye, let us hope she took after her mother," Aedan winked.

Weylyn laughed and swung his arm around his son's shoulders. "You get your looks from me, donnae be forgetting it, lad."

"Aye, but I donnae think a lass would appreciate it," he winked again. They all chuckled but soon the mood turned somber as Dagda turned back to his grove.

"I can only apologize for not being here and preventing the horror you all went through. The only consultation I have is, you are hale and hearty. Seanach and Bellegrid were unattached and had no lovers apart from who the gods decreed. They served me well and will be remembered for the warriors and heroes they were. Join me in remembering them and send them off with a warrior's blessing." All together the druids bent to the earth, grasped a handful of grass, ash, or char near them. Held it up over their heads and spoke together. *Fortuna mihi tete abstulitipsum quandoquidem. Atque in perpetuum, frater, ave atque vale.* Farewell."

They let what they were holding go as a strong wind blew through the area carrying some of the earth with it.

"You all have been given a gift from the gods, to leave this grove, marry who you choose, and all they ask is to continue the work you have done. The choice is yours," Dagda explained. "I journey to Alba to find my wife."

"All are welcome in my pack," Tristan stepped forward. "We would be honored if any of you would join us."

"Where in Alba?" someone questioned.

"On the mainland, a short journey to Skye. We are the Loch Alsh pack and settled near that water," Tristan answered.

"Search my memory, Remus. You will see and I place you, if you desire, as leader of those who wish to join," Dagda said. The druid named Remus, was quiet for a moment, eyes locked on Dagda, reading his thoughts.

"Aye, Alpha, I accept," Remus said. "I will join you. My sister is near there."

"Good, then anyone who desires to join us, please follow Remus," Tristan said.

"We will see you soon," Dagda replied. Then, with as light a heart as he had, Caylean journeyed back with them.

Caylean stopped at the gate of the Wolf Village and took a deep breath.

"I donnae think I can do this," he stated. Aedan stood before him and placed his hands on his son's shoulders. "I donnae deserve her."

"Nay, you donnae," Tristan stated from beside Dagda, his arms crossed over his chest. All eyes turned to him. He huffed a sigh. "But she is your mate. She chose you. And she carries your pup. I may no' like it, because of what you did, but I understand why you did it. Nae male is worthy of my daughter, but I will say, of anyone, I am glad 'tis you who stole her heart. After this eejit idea of yours to run from your problems I very much doubt you will ever leave her again. And I ken you love her. You would nae have sacrificed your life for her if you did nae. Believe me. I ken well. We all have learned something during this journey, and I have to say, I have learned what it means to be a better leader. I owe you an apology. You clearly did nae think you could come to me and I am sorry. I hope from now on, you will consider me as a friend and someone you can come to. That goes for all of you. I care for you, Caylean. But," he took a step closer to him. "If you ever hurt my daughter again, I will no' think twice of hurting you."

"I love you, son, but I will help him," Aedan replied.

"I would expect nae less," Caylean answered.

"Can we hurry?" Weylyn asked impatiently. "I have a mate and a daughter to see."

"Coming da'," Aedan called. "Let us go. She loves you son. She wants to be with you. But mark me, lad, you hurt your mother like that again, you and I will have more than just words. Understand?"

"Aye, da', I understand."

"And your wolf?" Dagda asked.

"I have nae heard him."

"He is still there, but will stay hidden, I would assume," Lucien replied. "He worries what you would do if he comes forward. It may take a little coaxing, but he will reappear. Now, let us go find your mate."

Chapter Sixteen

Giorsal stood on the small rise near the burn where the women washed clothes, staring out at the water. Her blonde hair lay loose about her and her arms wrapped around her body. She felt her mother come up beside her, but she said nothing.

"How are you feeling, my love?" Alexina asked.

"The pup is growing. It is strange, I have only been carrying for a couple weeks, but I felt him move."

"It was the same for me carrying you, Giorsal," she replied.

"And I miss my mate, Mama," she said. "I miss him so."

"I ken you do," Alexina replied. She turned her daughter toward her and framed her face. "You ken how much you are loved, aye? How much your father and I love you?"

"Aye," she answered. "And I love you and Papa, but I feel a part of me is missing."

"Perhaps that part of you is there?" Alexina indicated with her chin, behind her. Giorsal turned to look and saw Caylean standing on the green about fifty paces ahead of her. She gasped. Aedan and Weylyn hung back then, whispered something to Tristan, and Weylyn went to the keep. Giorsal locked eyes with her mate and watched as a myriad of emotions crossed his face. His chest heaved and she saw tracks of tears on his cheeks.

"Caylean?" She breathed. He took two steps toward her, then stopped. His chest heaved again but this time she rushed to him. Before she reached him, he lowered to his knee and bowed his head. She came to a stop before him.

"Mistress," he began. "I donnae deserve your forgiveness. I abandoned you and our child," his voice cracked. "But I swear to you before the gods, and your father, my alpha, I will never leave again. I will never hurt you and I will strive every day to be worthy of the precious gift of your love. If you will have me as your mate again."

He had not raised his eyes to her since he knelt to one knee. After a moment of silence, she reached forward and placed her hand on his hair. He looked up at her, his face streaked with tears.

"You have always and will always be my mate, Caylean," her voice was strong and loving. "And now before the gods, and my alpha I claim you as my mate again. I love you."

Caylean let out a soft moan and leaned forward, touching his forehead to her abdomen, completely unable to stand, his legs boneless. She held his head to her and let out a cry as she embraced her husband. Caylean wept into the folds of her gown and softly pressed his lips to the tiny bump he felt. Looking up at her, she grinned through her tears and knelt with him.

"Are you all right?" he asked. She nodded. "I am unsure how this happened."

"Nae son of mine would be unsure how that happened," Aedan teased.

"I am fairly certain he knows well," Dagda replied.

Caylean ignored them and gently touched his wife's stomach. "I had the spell."

"I have spoken with Agora," Giorsal revealed. "She said, due to you being a wolf hybrid and me being your true mate it may no' matter if you had a spell or no'."

"And you are all right with this?" he asked.

"Och aye," she answered. She took his face in her hands. "But, my mate, I have one request."

"Name it."

"I have been too long without your kiss," she said.

"Allow me to remedy that, my love," he leaned forward and kissed her.

Weylyn made his way up the back stair. Hurrying down the hall, he paused for a moment outside his chamber door. The fear of losing his mate was still raw but knowing she was well and just beyond the door made his hand twitch with the anticipation. Finally, he reached forward, and swung the door open.

His eyes darted around the room and fell on the bed. Eithne looked up at the intrusion as she nursed their pup.

Labhaoise snapped around from the fireplace, about to yell at who came in unannounced. But when she saw it was Weylyn, she smiled and snuck out of the room via the side door. Weylyn's eyes never left the baby. Eithne said nothing as she watched her mate stare at their daughter. Finally, he shuffled toward the bed and sat down beside her.

"You are well?" he asked looking up at his wife.

"After the hold was lifted, I was able to deliver our child free of complication. I am well, Weylyn," she said.

He tucked a piece of her hair back behind her ear and smiled as he kissed her. Eithne lifted their child a little higher in her arms. The tiny lass finally asleep and wrapped in a plaid.

"What have you named her?" Weylyn asked, as he gently stroked her soft cheek.

"I have nae," she answered. "I wanted to give you that honor."

She offered their child to him and tenderly, he took her in his arms. She did not wake as her father rocked her, humming. After a moment, Eithne cupped his jaw and wiped the tear that fell. He looked at her and grinned.

"What song do you sing?"

"The Wolf and the Willow Tree," he said. "My mother sang it to me as a pup."

"You miss her?"

"Every son misses their mother when they hold their child."

"What was her name?"

"Kyna," he answered and at that moment, their daughter opened her eyes and looked up at her father. "Kyna... so be it. A beautiful name for my beautiful lass."

"Kyna," Eithne smiled. "Aye, a perfect name for our lass."

Weylyn leaned toward her and kissed her softly. "I thank you, my love for this wonderful gift you have given me."

"You are welcome, Weylyn. I do love carrying your pups, but perhaps we can place the spell back on me? For I find this ordeal has made me leery of hurting a child."

"I agree to whatever you desire, my love. Have you tested to be sure she is well? After the scare with healing Aedan and the spell by Biróg?"

"She is fine," Eithne stated. "I believe. I hope."

"I am sure our lass is just fine," he answered and kissed her once more, but as soon as he looked back down at Kyna, her eyes flashed to the yellow of a wolf, then back to brown.

Eithne covered her mouth as a cry escaped. Weylyn froze. "There now, my little lass, tell your wolf she will be able to come out and play soon, but until then, we want to spend time with you." Her eyes flashed again then Kyna squirmed in his arms, snuggling tighter against her father and fell back asleep.

"I did nae think babes could have wolf eyes," Eithne said.

"They cannae," Weylyn answered. "'Tis a good thing Lucien is here. I will ask him. I have only heard of it happening once."

"When?"

"A wolf pup blessed by the Fae. The strongest of all. That pup became a great king who reigned over the natives of Alba for over one hundred years. Our lass is destined for greatness, Eithne."

"When the spell was lifted, I needed some time to recover and asked Blane to wait to tell you until the lass was cleaned and I had a chance to feed her, but..."

"How long?"

"It was only two hours," she replied.

"Two hours?" he questioned.

"Donnae be angry," she said.

"I am no'," he assured. "But we had only defeated Biróg moments before Tristan heard Blane's howl."

Eithne looked down at their child then back up at Weylyn. "I felt the spell lift as clear as if I was carrying a heavy burden. Do you think?"

"I will ask, but it is possible Kyna lifted it."

"How? She is but a pup?"

"That is a question we donnae have the answers to, my love. But let us thank the gods for this precious gift and let us be together as a family for a time. Then, I will discover what our lass truly is. I promise you."

Eithne agreed, leaned her head against Weylyn's shoulder, and watched her daughter, listening to Weylyn humming.

Chapter Seventeen

Dagda and Lucien walked with Tristan and Alexina through the village. Wolves and Druids greeted them. Two women passed in front of them and Lucien nudged his son.

"Agora!" Dagda called. She turned to look at him, her brow furrowed, but soon recognition crossed her face.

"Dagda?" she questioned. Myrna rushed to her son and embraced him.

"Aye," he answered and after his mother went to Lucien, he walked over to Agora.

"But how?" she asked, her fingers ghosting over his eyes, there was no scar nor any markings. He looked very different but still handsome to her.

"I... passed out of this world for a short time," he

explained and captured her hands in his as worry entered her eyes. "The gods granted me a new life, thanks to my father, but they also… Agora, they gave me my life back…" he breathed a laugh. "It is odd to see you with both eyes, but it only makes you twice as beautiful." She smiled at him but held his gaze. "I… ehm… they have released me and our grove from our pledge of never to mate."

"They have?"

"Aye… I was hoping… ehm," he cleared his throat.

"Come along, lad," Lucien called. "You did nae get this hesitation from me!"

"For shame, Lucien, shh," Myrna reproached.

Dagda breathed an uncomfortable laugh but raised her hands to his chest.

"What I am trying to say, Agora," he began again. "Will you by my mate? They have released us and given their consent. I love you and I will be a loyal to – mphm –" he was cut off by Agora throwing her arms around his neck and kissing him.

"Aye," she finally said pulling back. "I will marry you." Dagda grinned and kissed her once more. "When?"

"Right now," he replied.

"Now?"

"Woman, I have been waiting lifetimes to have you by my side properly. Aye, right now. Father, will you marry us?"

"With pleasure, son," Lucien called. "But you must allow her to prepare, as is our custom." Dagda growled, pulling her tighter to him.

"Give me an hour," Agora stated.

"No longer," Dagda ordered.

"Since your grove is free and some of your people will soon join us, I request you, your bride, and your parents stay with us for any length of time. We can rule together, if that is agreeable for I have nae right to lead druids. You will be their leader and I leader of the wolves."

"Aye, Alpha," Dagda replied. "I would enjoy that. I will yield to you as Alpha. I will be no threat to your leadership. Together we will make the way better for our people."

"'Tis glad I am," Tristan offered his arm in a warrior's shake. Dagda took it and locked eye with him. "I look forward to ruling by your side, brother."

"And I yours," Dagda answered. "If I may request one of my druids as my lieutenant?"

"Of course, which?"

"Remus. He has been by my side since I was a lad. We were born within a month of each other. He is a strong druid and loyal."

"I agree," Tristan acquiesced. "But I also ask you take Caylean as your other."

"That was my other plan," Dagda agreed.

"After your mating ceremony, we will meet to discuss with our lieutenants and my War Chief. We will outline plans and prepare for the journey ahead. Together."

"Aye," Dagda agreed. "But today I desire to take a mate."

"And I donnae wish to stop you," Tristan grinned. "Welcome and my best wishes for your future and happiness."

Myrna stepped forward. "It appears you both have a number of plans to make. I will gather our women to assist in your preparations, Agora," Myrna said. "Let us allow the men to speak. Come with me, child."

Agora thanked Myrna and, with a final look at Dagda, she smiled and left to prepare for her mating ceremony.

And as the sun set, Dagda and Agora were mated and Caylean and Giorsal renewed their vows. There was a grand celebration in the Great Hall and as Weylyn looked around, his mate on one side and his son on the other, his mind drifted back to all that had happened to get them there. With thanks and love in his heart, he took his wine goblet, raised it to the sky and drank.

End of Part One

Part Two

Chapter One

The door burst open, and Weylyn's moment of reprieve was shattered as he joined the warriors, standing and half phasing. Dagda and Lucien stood in front of the wolves, staring at the doorway that remained empty.

Aedan's nostrils flared and he immediately phased back to his human form. "Humans... Chief," he said softly to Tristan, but loudly enough wolf hearing caught what he said. The wolves phased back and pulled out their swords from their hiding places. Humans knew nothing of the pack and though Tristan was more than happy trading with them, after the betrayal of the MacRae clan, the pack treaded carefully.

Finally, a man entered, followed by three others. All

similarly dressed as peasant farmers, but Weylyn saw by the way they all carried themselves, they were far from farmers.

"Welcome... friends," cautiously, Tristan stepped forward in greeting. "I am Tristan, Chief and Leader of this clan. I am sure you are welcome. What brings you out on such a dismal night?"

One of the men pulled off his cloak and handed it to another in his group. "Our thanks, Chief," he said. His voice distinctly Highlander. "We have journeyed far. Forgive us for imposing. We saw the lights and were hoping for a safe place to outstay the storm. We only ask for a few hours, until the storm passes."

"You are welcome," Tristan announced. "We are celebrating two unions this eve. Please join us for some food and ale. What are your names?"

"Och, forgive our discourteousness. I am Diarmad," he answered. "This is my wife and brother along with our friend. We travel north back to our lands but were waylaid by the deluge." He shook out his tunic to show how wet it was.

"It is quite a storm, to be sure," Tristan replied. The remaining three took off their cloaks.

Aedan stiffened beside his father and Weylyn looked over at him, his eyes on one of the other men. The human was no older than the human age of thirty-six. The man gasped when he locked eyes with him.

"Aedan?" he breathed. Aedan's breath hitched for a moment, then his eyes shadowed, and his face grew stern.

"Do I ken you, sir? For I donnae ken an Aedan," he replied.

"Forgive me," the man said. "You look so like someone I once kenned as a boy."

"Brother?" the Diarmad cautioned.

"It is all well, Diar," he answered. "I feel nae animosity

here. Do you Aileas?" He turned to the dark-haired woman beside him. She shook her head but her green eyes were on Isla, Eithne, and Agora. "Forgive the pretense, Chief," he continued, looking back at Tristan. "I am Nairn, Chief of the Farquharsons. We travel back northeast from visiting my sister on her wedding. My brother is War Chief of our clan and he desires to keep us as you see, only farmers as to no' draw attention. I thought I kenned your man, but clearly, I am mistaken. Though..." he sighed harshly, looking at Aedan again. "You look so like my father's War Chief and dearest friend. May I ask, what is your name?"

"Gowan," Aedan answered quickly.

"That was the name of his father," Nairn said. "Who is your father?"

"Am I to be subjected to these questions by a guest?" Aedan demanded.

"Bring food and ale," Tristan ordered one of the servants. "Let us sit."

"I am sorry if I offended your man, Chief," Nairn spoke low as he and Tristan walked to the dais. "It took me by surprise."

"Gowan is my War Chief," Tristan said using the name Aedan chose. "He is cautious just like your brother."

"The man I kenned was very dear to me, like a father," Nairn explained. "I see it now, he cannae be him. Aedan would never be so... heartless."

Aedan turned on his heels and walked out of the room. He could not let Nairn, a boy dear enough to him to call a son, see him. Nor could he hear Nairn dismiss him so. Weylyn followed him down the corridor and into another room, far away from the Great Hall. Weylyn shut the door and placed a hand on his son's shoulder, feeling the shaking of his barely suppressed emotions. Aedan finally turned to him. Anger, fear, sadness, and pain all washed over him. Weylyn soothed his hair and pulled him close.

When Aedan pulled back, he wiped a hand down his face. "Forgive me," he said.

"Nay, there is nothing to forgive," Weylyn assured.

"'Tis just... before Isla and I were married, I did nae think I would ever have a family or children. Nairn was born to Sheiling, my dearest friend. I taught him how to fight, how to use a sword. He was like a son to me. Sheiling was my brother in all ways. I was his *Tanist*, his heir, second-in-command, but when Nairn was born, it was a joyous time for us both. Him, as the father and me, as, well... an uncle, brother, comrade. It was difficult to define our relationship as we were nae blood but closer than. To lie to that boy... to dismiss him as I did, was a disrespect to his father."

"I had such a relationship with Faolán," Weylyn replied. "His pups would have been as mine, as mine would have been as his. Unfortunately, neither of us were blessed to see each other's offspring in person. But I do understand what you are describing. Blood of bone instead of blood of blood."

"'Tis exactly that," Aedan agreed. "I have never forgiven myself for just leaving his clan... Sheiling, without explanation. I..." he looked down. "I asked Isla to assist me once, without Tristan's knowledge. She was able to project my image and I was able to speak with him. I told him everything and begged him on our friendship, to stop looking for me. He agreed but told me to come back. He did nae care I was a wolf. He simply wanted his friend back. I could nae. I will always regret no' seeing him once more before he died."

"You have a chance to look after his son for him," Weylyn stated. "Even for a day."

"How, da'? How?" he asked. "The man he kenned is gone. How am I to explain what and who I am now? No' only that, Tristan would never agree. I have already betrayed him once by telling Sheiling everything, I could nae do so again."

"Talk to him," Weylyn replied. "He is nae a tyrant. He would understand."

"Would he?" He asked. "He has nae had that sort of friendship."

"Is there nae one he has grown close to? Someone he calls upon for council and merely to talk? Come now, lad, you ken the truth."

"Me?" he asked.

"Of course."

"I had nae thought of that." Aedan sighed. The door opened and Caylean snuck in, quickly closing the door after him.

"Forgive me, da', *seanair*," he said. "Are you well?"

"Aye, lad, I thank you," Aedan answered.

"I felt your pain and I could nae take it away from you," Caylean explained. "My powers... have nae returned. I am sorry."

"I thank you, but I am well. 'Twas a shock to be sure. He was like a son to me before you were born. His father was a good friend and he looks so like his da'," Aedan shook his head. "Of course for him to remember me..."

"Tristan asked me to tell you, he is sorry to have invited them to stay but he could do nothing else," Caylean relayed.

"Highland Hospitality," Aedan nodded. "And if he turned them out, they would find it suspicious. It is well. We must go before we are missed."

"We should have a name for your father and mother should they ask again," Weylyn said.

"Weylyn works for me," Aedan answered.

"Aye, and for me," Weylyn teased. "But what about your mother. You took Gowan's name, rightly so, but if you say Brietta, he will remember."

"If he asks, I will think of something," Aedan said. "Let us go."

Tristan watched his two dearest friends leave the room. He saw Aedan's pain and remembered their many shared confidences about what Aedan called his *previous life*, the time before he knew he was wolf.

As the servants placed a tray of food before their guests, Tristan sat beside Nairn and discretely watched the chief. Aedan had told him stories of the might of the Farquharson clan and the joy of being the chief's closest friend. Nairn, the chief next to him, had been a boy when Aedan left to help Weylyn fight Marrock and free Tristan from his father's clutches. Now thirty years later, Aedan looked the same, but the boy was grown and Sheiling, Nairn's father was long dead. The pain Aedan felt was palpable and as Alpha, Tristan felt it as if it was his own.

When Caylean passed him, he reached out to stop him. The chief, distracted by Alexina asking after his family, paid no attention.

"Please, go to your father. Tell him I am sorry, but I have to have them stay."

"I will," Caylean whispered and followed Aedan and Weylyn down the corridor.

"Tell me, Chief," Tristan turned to his guests. "Where is Farquharson land?"

"Northeast about two days' ride," he explained. "Just near the great loch, Ness."

"I ken it well," Tristan wished he could call back the words as soon as he said them. The area was near enough to his father's lands.

"Indeed? How so?" Diarmad asked.

"I have traveled much before settling here," Tristan answered.

"So, you are nae an established clan?" Diarmad replied.

"We are for the last ten years," he shorted the time, due to him looking the same age as the two men beside him.

"What name do you go by?" Nairn asked.

"Mac... Kinnon," he answered. "We are the MacKinnons."

"Your father?" Nairn asked.

"Aye," Tristan lied. "A great man."

"You have amassed quite a clan following in a short decade, Chief," Diarmad observed.

"We are fortunate," Tristan replied.

"A word, if I may, Chief," Dagda said walking up the dais and bowing.

"Ah, of course. Do excuse me," Tristan stood and stepped away from their guests.

Weylyn, Aedan and Caylean entered the room but before they could join them, Dagda led Tristan to them.

"What is it?" Tristan asked.

"She is a druid," Dagda replied, his eyes on the woman, Aileas, seated beside Diarmad.

"You are certain?" Aedan asked. "The Farquharsons would nae have a druid in their midst. They did nae believe in it."

"Aye, positive," Dagda answered. "Both my father and I felt her energy."

"I am curious why they were drawn here," Weylyn said.

"The lad knew you, Aedan?" Dagda asked. "It would save time if you allow me to read your mind." Aedan nodded. They were silent for a moment as Dagda gathered the information he sought. "I see. I do believe it was this lad's connection to you as a friend and mentor that drew them here. She leads them, not the brother. Beware of her. I cannot discern her true purposes. They could be nothing and they could be malicious."

"We will beware," Tristan promised and before they drew suspicion, headed back to his guests. Aedan, Weylyn and Caylean following.

"You said you were celebrating two unions this eve, Chief," Nairn said. "Forgive us for interrupting. We just returned from my sister's nuptials."

"Indeed, two of my warriors were gifted with their brides this very day," Tristan answered. "Well, one was returning to her after a long time apart. But we celebrate their reunion as well as another's. From where have you journeyed?"

"We came from the Isles," Nairn replied. "She made an advantageous marriage to the Maclean chief."

"We heard about some... unpleasantness near here, Chief," Diarmad said. "Something to do with wild animals in the area. Wolves."

"Aye," Tristan replied. "I heard about it too. Some MacRaes were killed. We have nae been bothered."

"My brother's betrothed had a death in her family," Diarmad revealed. "Her brother and heir to the MacRae chiefdom."

"I heard and paid my respects to the chief myself," Tristan replied. "I am sorry for your betrothed's loss."

Nairn waved him off. "I am sorry to say, it was nae a love match," he answered. "And it is over now, anyway."

"You are nae married?" Aedan asked.

Nairn did not look at him for a moment then finally turned to him. "Nay, this was to be my first marriage. I could nae subject her to a life of marital... tolerance. My own father had an arranged marriage and he did nae love his wife."

"That is nae true, Shieling loved—" Aedan bit his tongue.

"You kenned my father... how?" Nairn's face hardened.

Aedan swallowed but attempted to salvage. "I merely... I heard most arranged marriages end in love."

Nairn said nothing for a long moment. "'Tis possible," he finally replied. "And my father did love his wife, but she died in childbirth with my sister, our youngest sibling. My father never recovered after his dearest friend left without explanation and then his wife died. He was a broken shell of his former self by the time death took him."

Aedan never dropped Nairn's gaze but after a moment, he stood. "I am to take the next watch. If you forgive me, Chief."

Tristan nodded and watched him go. "We will nae trespass on your time for much longer, Chief. We thank ye for your hospitality. It looks as if the storm is breaking."

"You are welcome," Tristan said. "But it is dark and late. Perhaps you would honor us by staying the night. Start fresh in the morning."

"We would nae wish to intrude," Nairn replied.

"Nay intrusion," Tristan answered. "I insist. We–"

At that moment, the door opened, and Blane walked in. Not unusual since he was coming in after Aedan relieved him of his watch, but what caused the ruckus from their guests was, Blane had not phased. His brown wolf stood on all fours, standing well over eight feet tall. The massive creature saw the guests and Tristan's wide eyes, barked an apology, and rushed out of the great hall, knocking over a table of ale in his haste.

Nairn and Diarmad stood and pulled their dirks from their sheaths. "What, in the name of the gods, was that?" Diarmad demanded, looking at Tristan for explanation.

"My pet." Tristan's smooth lie sent a shiver of memory down Weylyn's spine. His cool mask of indifference, as he leaned back in his chair and twirled his own dirk between his hand, reflected his father. Marrock's shadow passed over him but Weylyn tempered his immediate reaction.

"That was a wolf demon," Diarmad stated.

"He is a wolfman, aye, but he is hardly a demon," Tristan's voice mimicked the disinterested tone he had heard his father use on so many occasions. "In fact, he is one of my prized possessions. He is a good warrior, but after I killed his mate, he was my slave. He will do anything I ask." The story made up as he went, Tristan saw Odara, Blane's mate glance his way.

"He is a danger," Diarmad replied.

"He is nae a danger," Tristan answered.

"Could he have nae been the one to kill the MacRae heir?" Nairn asked, surprising Tristan with his interest, instead of the hostility Diarmad so neatly portrayed.

"He did nae kill the MacRae heir," Tristan said. "As I said, he is my pet and I keep him for my own enjoyment. Sometimes, I have him fight others of his kind and sometimes, I use him as my executioner. I cannae tell you how interesting it is to watch them fighting. It is very amusing. Now, let us have music, dancing, and more ale."

"If you would be so kind, Chief," Nairn stopped the servant from refilling his cup. "I find I am very tired, from the journey. Do you think I could accept your generous offer of staying the evening?"

"Of course," Tristan answered. He snapped his fingers and another servant came forward. "Take the Chiefs Farquharson to the guest chambers above stairs."

"Our friend can stay with your men in the barracks," Nairn looked over at the man who travelled with them. He nodded.

"Nonsense," Tristan said. "We have plenty of room. Aileas, will you need a chamber of your own? Forgive me, I did nae ask if you were mated... married to one of them."

"I am no' married, Chief. Nor am I mated," she replied. "But I will stay with Diarmad, if that is acceptable to you."

"Perfectly fine, we had nae judgement here. In fact, our women are held to the same standards as our men. They chose who they want, no' the men."

"My thanks, Chief," she curtseyed. Tristan watched them leave then leaned over to Caylean.

"Find Blane, tell him to keep himself hidden, phase, and stay locked in his room," Tristan ordered. Caylean nodded, kissed Giorsal's hand and left the room. "Dagda, Lucien, do you think you could make them forget?"

"It would be difficult," Lucien said. "I may be able to cast a spell to have them think they dreamt it. But depending on the woman's hold on them and her powers, it may not have the desired outcome."

Tristan nodded. "Weylyn, find Aedan, tell him what happened. He needs to stay far enough away from them until they leave. I cannae have another slip up."

"Understood," Weylyn replied.

Taking a moment to shake off his father's persona, Tristan reached to grasp Weylyn's hand. "My thanks, my friend."

Weylyn nodded but left to find his son.

"I am sorry, my love," Tristan turned to his daughter. "This was nae the reunion I hoped for you nor the mating evening for you, Dagda. I am sorry for it."

"Dearest Papa," Giorsal covered his hand. "Donnae worry. All will be well. It is more important to protect the pack."

"Aye," Dagda replied. "My father and I will stay awake throughout the evening to make certain all is well."

"Nay, you will not, lad," Lucien answered. "Your mother and I have been waiting a millennium for you to give us grandpups. You and Agora will consummate your mating. I will remain vigilant."

"Da'," Dagda stated, even though he glanced at Agora who smiled and looked down as a blush colored her cheeks.

"No question, lad," Lucien said. "Now, take your bride and go. We have this well in hand."

"Indeed," Tristan agreed. "My thanks. Enjoy your evening." Dagda looked at Agora who stood and offered her hand to him. Once they left, Tristan turned to his daughter.

"Take to your room, my sweet one. Bar the door. Rest."

"I thank you, Papa," she said. "I am tired of late."

"With good reason," he glanced down at her stomach the tiny bump hidden beneath the folds of her gown. "Sleep well."

She kissed his forehead as she stood. The door opened and Caylean walked back in, nodding to Tristan. Giorsal met her mate near the stairs and told him what had happened. Caylean stroked her cheek, kissed her softly and watched her take the stairs to their chamber, then he strode over to Tristan.

"Blane has phased, and he snuck up the back stairs. He is in his room," Caylean explained.

"My thanks, Caylean," Tristan replied. "And Aedan?"

"He and *Seanair* are speaking on the battlements," Caylean said.

"Good, then go to your mate, Caylean," he ordered. "We have this well in hand."

"You are sure I can be of nae assistance?" Caylean asked.

"Nay," Tristan replied. "I thank you. I need you to protect my daughter."

"With my life," Caylean swore. Bowing once to his alpha, he said good night to his mother and the others before heading up the stairs.

"I will stay with you, Alpha," Lucien offered sitting beside him.

"My thanks, Lucien," Tristan said. "I will nae seek my bed tonight."

"Nor I," the dark druid agreed.

"I will also stay if it is acceptable, Alpha," Bowdyn stepped forward.

"Aye, my thanks, Bowdyn. Alexina, Myrna, Isla, Eithne, Labhaoise, please retire to your rooms and bar the door. Allow none but your mates entrance."

"Have nae fear of us, Alpha," Isla said. "We have taken care of ourselves before."

"We will bar ourselves in my solar, my love," Alexina said as the women gathered their food and goblets of wine. "Come to us when all is well."

"I will," Tristan answered. The women left the hall and the servants cleared the table. Tristan, Lucien, and Bowdyn moved to the chairs beside the fire. Sitting together, they kept their ears tuned to the stairs. Weylyn soon joined them and together they waited for the sun to rise and their unexpected guests to be on their way.

But somewhere in the back of his mind, Tristan knew they had yet to see the last of the Farquharsons and their druid.

Chapter Two

Aedan walked down the corridor, silently. The moon was high in the sky and the stars twinkled brightly. It was well past the witching hour and though the keep seemed asleep, the warrior within him knew it was merely a façade and was waiting for the sun to rise.

"You always did walk the halls at night," a voice said from one of the rooms. "I remember how you and father used to walk together."

Aedan froze but eventually turned around to see Nairn standing, arms crossed, in the doorway of a guest room.

"I ken no' what you mean," Aedan said.

"Drop the pretense, Aedan. I ken 'tis you," Nairn replied. "I have nae figured out how, but I ken 'tis you."

"My name is nae Aedan," he stated.

"Aye, 'tis," Nairn stepped into the hallway. "Gowan was your father. Do you think I have forgotten? Twas easy for you to say his name as it is a name you would ken and answer to. But that is nae your name. And the Aedan I kenned… would never lie to me."

"The Aedan you kenned is dead," Aedan replied.

"Perhaps," Nairn answered, taking another step closer to him. "But you are the Aedan I kenned once. Whether he is dead and gone, I donnae care. The man my father cared for, the man I care for, he is still in you."

Aedan looked away when Nairn reached him and they stood nearly eye to eye, Aedan's wolf height giving him a slight advantage.

"What happened to you? How are you here? How do you look the same?" Nairn asked.

"I… I donnae ken what you mean," Aedan said. "I am nae this Aedan."

Nairn said nothing for a long moment but held his gaze. "My father spent years searching for you. He nearly died of exposure while climbing the mountain near our home thinking perhaps you had taken an early walk. He hid it, but he mourned you. He cried once to me. And then mother died… It broke him. You broke him."

"I did nae," Aedan breathed. "I could nae."

"You did," Nairn replied. "He was never the same after you left… *I* was never the same. One day you were there, helping me, teaching me, being a second father to me and then the next… I went out that morning so excited. You were going to teach me how to throw a spear. You said I was ready. I remember. I ran to see you, only to find the bailey empty. My father, beside himself with fear for you and your family. Granted, we had seen less and less of you since your mother died. Father said you needed to mourn, but you promised to be back. You swore to me; I could always rely on you."

"You can."

"Then where were you?" Nairn bellowed. "Where were you when my father got sick? Where were you when my mother died? Where were you when my father died? Where were you when I needed you? Where were you?"

Aedan stared into his eyes seeing the years of pain and sadness. They reflected his own emotions and the only thing Aedan could do, was reach for him. Without thought, Aedan grabbed Nairn to him and held him tightly. Nairn pushed away from him and took two steps back. Aedan let the pain dissipate.

"Tell me who you are. Tell me you are him," Nairn begged, his voice cracking. "I need you to be him."

Aedan closed his eyes for a moment, but finally opened them and stared at the man he remembered as a boy. The one who would run to him the moment he left the keep and throw his arms around his neck. The one who would stare in awe as he and Shieling sparred. The one he taught to ride a horse, hold a sword, carve a bow. The boy he would carry on his shoulders through the village just so he could get a piece of warm bread before it cooled in the Northern Highland air. The boy who loved him. The boy he loved as a son. The man he grew into. The man before him.

"Nair," he breathed. "I am sorry."

Nairn's breath hitched. "Say it."

Aedan closed his eyes, unable to see the hatred in Nairn's eyes. Slowly, he nodded and, taking a deep breath, he opened his eyes again. "I have missed you and your father for decades, Nairn. Aye, 'tis me. I cannae tell you how, or why, or what happened. But 'tis me, lad."

Nairn stared at him, his chest heaved, but he could not get a deep breath. "Why?" was all he could say. Aedan closed his eyes again and looked away. "Look at me, damn you! I think I deserve an explanation."

"You do," Aedan agreed. "But that is something I cannae give."

"Why?"

"It is nae my secret," Aedan explained.

"You left my father to die a lonely old man when you were here all along, you selfish bastard."

"Aye, and if I had kenned, I would have come see him."

"I would nae let you in," Nairn sneered.

"With good reason," Aedan replied. "And I cannae ask your forgiveness, because it is clear you donnae want to give it. I cannae blame you for that. But I can tell you, no' a day went by when I did nae mourn what I had lost. No' a day went by, when I did nae think of you and your father. No' a day went by. So call me anything. Call me selfish, call me whatever you please, but ken this lad, no' a day, an hour, a moment went by when I did nae think of all I left behind. And when I found out your father died; I was gutted. I wanted to go to you. I wanted to help you in any way I can, but I could no'."

"Why? What does this chief have on you? Why are you a slave here?"

"I am no' a slave," Aedan disagreed. "I hold the same position here as I held with your father."

"So we were nae good enough for you?"

"Nay, that is no' it," Aedan replied.

"Then what?"

"'Tis complicated," Aedan answered.

"I am a smart man," Nairn stated. "I believe I can understand." Aedan shook his head and turned from him. "Nay, donnae turn from me. You donnae get to turn from me." Nairn rushed to him and grabbed his arm, ripping him back around to face him. Aedan could not control it, and his eyes changed to the yellow of his wolf. Nairn's eyes grew large as he stepped back. Aedan looked away and closed his eyes for a moment, only to turn back with his eyes back to the brown of his human. "What are you?" Nairn breathed. Aedan took a deep breath and let it out harshly.

"I am a wolf," he said simply.

It took a moment but Nairn stepped toward him, concern written all over his face. "Dear gods, were you bitten?"

"Nay," Aedan shook his head.

"What then?" he asked.

Sighing again, he looked down the corridor to be sure no one was there and then turned back to Nairn. "My mother was mated to a wolfman before she married the man who raised me. She was mated to a man named Weylyn, you saw him this evening. He was the one sitting beside me. She was mated to him and fully expected to live long with him, but his alpha was a tyrant and refused the match. They were forbidden to see each other again. Gowan was my mother's dearest friend and when she discovered she was expecting a child; he married her and raised me as his own. The time my mother died, we were attacked by wolves sent by the alpha and my mother was killed, but before she died, she told me of my true sire. Weylyn was there and during the month I was mourning my mother, we stayed at her cottage and Weylyn taught me how to phase. When I was prepared, we left to save Weylyn's alpha, Tristan."

"Tristan?" Nairn asked.

"Aye, the Tristan you met. He was in his father's clutches and was being tortured. We went to save him and..."

"And?" Nairn prompted.

"We did, but I realized I was affected by wolf's bane and could nae longer be around it. Then, something else happened that I cannae tell you but needless to say, it changed me again. I kenned then, I could never go back, nae matter how much I wanted to. I have been with the pack ever since. But I have missed you."

Nairn said nothing for a long moment, then finally, "did da' ken this?"

"Aye," Aedan replied. "I was able to tell him."

"How?"

"My wife," Aedan admitted.

"Isla?" Nairn questioned. "What about her?"

Aedan thought about lying to him, telling him she had family in the area, and they got a message to Shieling, but he knew Nairn would never forgive him if he lied again. And the memory of the woman travelling with them came back to Aedan.

"She is a Druid High Priestess," Aedan stated. "She projected my image to Sheiling, and I was able to speak with him."

Nairn studied him for a long moment. Aedan never dropped his gaze but after a full two minutes passed, he huffed and looked down.

"You are immortal," Nairn finally said. Aedan looked back up at him surprised, but he schooled his features. "That is why you never returned. You are immortal now. You look the same as you always did."

"Aye," he eventually agreed. "'Tis a curse or a gift we were given. But it is something I have loathed several times these past thirty-odd years. I have lost many people I hold dear, your father being one of them. But I am with my family and my pack."

Nairn nodded slowly. "Da's final words make sense now."

"What did he say?"

"He said, 'immortals ken more pain than all the world combined. You will join me someday, somehow, but pity those who never can.' He kenned what you were."

"I told him," Aedan admitted. "But he swore he would never tell, and he stopped looking for me."

"I remember that day, he called off the search, proclaiming you were dead."

"In a way I was," he replied. "As I said earlier, the Aedan you kenned is dead."

"You are right," Nairn answered. "Because the Aedan I kenned would never leave his friends. I mourned that man. You... are no' him. You could never be him. I am glad when the sun comes up, I will never have to see you again."

"Nairn," he stepped forward.

"Nay," he moved back. "Leave me in peace, as you did all those years ago. I meant so little to you then, I must mean nothing to you now. As you mean to me." He turned and walked back into his room, shutting the door.

Aedan felt the tears on his cheeks as the door shut and he heard the muffled sound of the bar being lowered into place. The final goodbye, he would never forget.

Chapter Three

"Alpha," Aedan's voice came from the stairs. Tristan, Weylyn, Lucien, and Bowdyn turned to him. His father stood and immediately went to him, when he saw the look in his eyes.

"Aedan, what is wrong?" Tristan asked.

"I have come to you now before the sun rises. I ask you to punish me before my mate awakens."

"Punish you?" Weylyn and Tristan both questioned.

"What is going on?" Tristan continued.

"I... I have betrayed you," Aedan said.

"I find that hard to believe," Tristan stated.

"It is true," he replied. "For I have revealed what I am."

"That was my father's law, no' mine, Aedan. Come sit with us, tell us what happened."

Aedan fell into the chair Weylyn offered and dropped his head into his hands.

"Forgive me, Alpha," he said. "But I was… Nairn cornered me in the hallway. I tried to brush him off, but he would nae stop. I could nae stop myself, he grabbed me and when I turned to him, my eyes were…"

"That of a wolf?" Weylyn asked gently.

"Aye, and then I could nae hide any longer. It all came pouring out." Aedan looked to Tristan. "I am sorry. He was like a son to me and I could nae lie to him."

"And his reaction?" Tristan asked calmly.

"He was angry I never told him and that I left both he and his father. But I betrayed you, Alpha. By telling him and putting us all in danger. I am sorry."

Tristan was silent for a long moment. Weylyn held his son's arm, watching Tristan. Finally, the alpha stood and walked to the fire.

"The lad means a great deal to you, Aedan. I felt your pain," Tristan revealed. "With that said, there is nae punishment I could mete out that would be worse than the punishment you are putting yourself through. With that said, you must ken I have a duty to punish you for making us vulnerable." Tristan sighed and turned to face him. "You will take an extra watch and perimeter run every night for a moon's cycle, that is your punishment."

"'Tis too lenient, Alpha," Aedan said. "For it was no' the first time I betrayed you."

"Indeed?" Tristan raised his brows.

"I also told Shieling many years ago. It was to stop him from looking for me. I needed to tell him I was well."

Tristan was quiet. "And how were you able to tell him? Did you send a message?"

"In a way," Aedan admitted. "Isla projected my image and I was able to speak with him. He was looking for me and I needed to tell him to stop. My wife did as I asked, please donnae punish her."

"I could nae punish either of you, my friend," Tristan replied. "I can understand your need to tell your dearest friend you were well." His eyes drifted to Weylyn. "Or to make sure he is well and your foolishness of running away did not allow him to be harmed. Be at ease. All will be well."

"I thank you, Tristan," Aedan said. "He was like a brother to me."

"I ken what that is like," Tristan answered, his eyes still on Weylyn.

"We all do," Lucien replied.

"I will tell Blane to add me to the rotation," Aedan said turning to go. "If anything happens because I told him…"

"Nothing will happen," Weylyn assured. "Now, join us and speak nae more on it."

Aedan looked back at them, nodded in thanks, and accepted a cup of whisky from Tristan. Together they sat before the fire, silent but ever watchful.

Nairn paced in his room. The fire was lit and provided the only light. The pain was so great he was not certain if it was hurt or anger. Many times, they were similar. His thoughts turned to his father and how he changed overnight. One day, he demanded nearly every able-bodied man to go out looking for Aedan, then the next, called them all back and proclaimed Aedan was dead. But during the weeks that followed, he had called upon the Druids near them to rejoin the clan. They had been banished by Nairn's great-grandfather when St. Columba journeyed to Alba from Erin in the mid-fifth century, spreading

Christianity. But after Nairn's father welcomed them back, the Farquharsons began to live at peace with them once more. His own brother had taken a druid mistress. Though her powers far exceeded Nairn's understand, he was grateful his brother understood.

She had been drawn to that place and Nairn realized why; Isla was a druid. Nairn tried to remember what Isla was like but all he could remember was, she looked like a goddess and he was as enthralled as any six-year-old boy would be.

He always wondered at his father's change. He had welcomed Druids back with open arms and had removed all wolf's bane from the village and keep. He claimed it was because it was no longer needed, that the wolf problem was over. But even then, Nairn wondered.

Now the bitter truth sat disgustingly on him and he took the chair by the bed. His father knew and never told him. When Shieling died, nearly ten years ago, Nairn had his time of mourning, made even stronger by the absence of his mother and Aedan. But he took hope in the fact his father loved him, he was with his mother, and possibly seeing Aedan again in whatever heaven existed.

Now the truth was revealed and shattered his perfect little construct. His brother, who had been born after Aedan left was the only council he trusted, and he needed him.

Leaving the room, Nairn snuck out and down the two doors to where his brother slept. Though from the sounds drifting through the door, Diarmad was doing little sleeping. Still, needs must, and Nairn opened the door.

A squeal from the bed and his brother, far too slowly, got to his feet, grabbing his dagger off the side table.

Heaving breaths, Diarmad lowered the steel when he saw it was Nairn.

"God's bones, Nair," he breathed and looked over at the bed where Aileas held the sheet to her chest. "What, in the name of the gods, do you think you are doing?"

"Careful, remember to whom you speak, brother," Nairn replied. Diarmad moved to the chair beside the fire and pulled on his trousers. Still without his tunic, he turned back to his brother.

"I am ever your humble servant, dear Chief," mockingly, he bowed to him but one look at his brother's face gave him pause. "What is it?"

"I must speak with you," Nairn said.

"Very well," Diarmad took his dirk again and strapped it to his waist. Leaning over the bed, he kissed Aileas and left the room following his brother.

"What is the matter?" Diarmad asked as soon as the door was closed, and they stood in Nairn's room. For a brief moment, Nairn thought about not telling him. Diarmad was far too young and did not know Aedan. Though he remembered their father's grief, he did not understand why. But the moment was fleeting and Nairn soon turned to his War Chief.

"Do you recall father speaking of his War Chief? The one who died?"

Diarmad observed him. "Why do you say *died* with such blatant hostility?"

"Do you recall?" Nairn pressed, ignoring his brother's question.

"Aye," he answered. "Da' mentioned him a few times while he was training me. Said he died in some attack. But he was the greatest War Chief he ever kenned. Why?"

"Because he did nae die. He is here, in this keep," Nairn said.

Diarmad raised an eyebrow and in that move, he looked just like their father. "Brother," he said cautiously. "It has been a long journey, you are tired, perhaps it would be best if you took to your bed."

"I am nae a child for you to coddle, brother," he spoke heatedly. "I ken who he is. He was Father's best friend. You were nae born yet. He is a wolf. They are all wolves here. Tristan is the alpha."

Diarmad did not look convinced. "Wolves are a thing of legend brother. They are nae real."

"And the beast we saw tonight? That was what? Looked fairly like a wolf to me. And the women? They are druids." When Diarmad did not speak for a time, Nairn looked over at him. "You kenned this."

His brother was always good at hiding his emotions, but Nairn had been able to read him since he was a lad. Diarmad looked over at him then away again. But eventually nodded. Nairn waited for him to explain.

"Aileas felt it earlier," he finally said. "She told me just a bit ago."

"And you were going to tell me... when? *After* you were finished whatever you were doing?" Nairn demanded.

"If you have to ask what we were doing, I worry for you, brother."

"Arse."

"Aye, was that supposed to be a shocking declaration there?" Diarmad questioned.

"What else did she tell you?" Nairn sighed.

"Nothing much. Just that she felt the druids were here and felt a power unlike she had ever felt."

"And why did you nae tell me the second she told you? That is your duty."

"I was taking care of other duties. I was a wee bit busy, if you had nae noticed there, brother."

"Aye, I did notice, and I noticed you refused to come to your chief with pertinent information."

"So punish me," Diarmad taunted. "I told you now. But what does it have to do with anything? Da' welcomed Druids back home so why are you worried about it?"

"You would nae understand."

"I might, if you actually gave me a chance to try and understand it."

Nairn was quiet for a time and Diarmad finally sighed. "If you want to tell me, come find me. But until then, I donnae wish to be standing here when there is a soft, warm lass waiting for me. But I have to say one thing. If da' cared for this man as much as you say, he would welcome him with open arms. He would be downstairs at this very moment speaking with him, catching up on the years lost between them. No' in his room, wallowing in his own self-pity, anger and hate. He would set it all aside and thank the gods for the reunion. Only a thought." Diarmad turned to the door.

"I hate you sometimes," Nairn muttered.

Diarmad froze but did not turn around. "Love you too, brother." With that, he left Nairn alone with his thoughts.

Chapter Four

"And you ken the funniest bit?" Aedan's speech was slurred with one too many whiskies. "The funniest bit is he had to run naked down the street because he did nae have time to get dressed..." he broke off into drunken giggles. "The lass's da' was chasing after him!" He barely got out, before more laughter escaped him. The others laughed good-naturedly knowing the reason behind Aedan's unusual excess drinking was to dull the ache of mourning. Tristan looked over at Weylyn who nodded.

Unbeknownst to Aedan, they had been watering down the alcohol and alternating between refilling his cup with whisky and water.

Aedan's laughter died and they looked over at him. He

was staring at the cup in his hand, then the fire beyond. "Dear gods, I miss him," his voice cracked with emotion. "I miss him." Aedan tossed back the whisky and stared into the fire.

Movement near the stairs caught their eye.

"He missed you too, Aedan," Nairn said. Aedan froze, then turned to his father. Weylyn's eyes were on the man behind him. Slowly, Aedan turned and saw Nairn waiting by the stairs. He stood suddenly, far too sober for the meeting. Though his mind cleared, his body weaved a moment and Lucien steadied him with a wave of his hand.

"Nairn, I ken you hate me, but you donnae ken the entire story. Time means little when you are immortal. I did nae realize how much time had passed until I was told he died. My one thought was you and how I could nae be there for you. I am sorry. I ken you never wanted to see me again. I will go and stay in my room until you leave."

He made a move to walk to the stairs but realized Nairn stood in the way. He waited awkwardly as no idea came to his still cloudy mind. Missing the look between his father and Lucien, he jumped when suddenly his head cleared, and body no longer felt the effects of the alcohol. Looking around the room, his eyes lightened on Lucien who nodded once.

"I was angry with you for so long," Nairn's voice brought Aedan back. "I hated you for leaving us... me. When my father died, I did nae have anyone to look up to. I survived and now seeing you again. I should be thankful, happy even, but my anger, something I had to hold tightly to, escaped and all those years of worry, pain, being afraid I would, *could* never lead my clan like my father, came pouring out. When you lied to me, then fell into my trap of when I said my parents never loved each other, I kenned it truly was you and everything I had tried so hard to hold inside, burst out. I regret what I said to you just a bit ago, it was said in anger. My brother helped me see that if da' was alive and he had been the one to see you, he would have greeted you with open arms. I wish to remedy that if you would allow me. I loved you as a second father, I should have embraced you as such." Nairn took a few steps, still cautious but Aedan met him halfway and they embraced tightly. "I am sorry, my friend."

"I cannae tell you how sorry I am, Nair," Aedan said. "I never wanted to leave, but I had nae choice. Once I kenned my true parentage, I wanted to help and then I was immortal. I could nae stay in one place, let alone go back to a place that kenned my age and me. But you both were never far from my thoughts and my heart."

"Nor you from ours," Nairn said.

"Please sit with us, let me introduce my father and alpha," Aedan offered. Nairn nodded and walked back with him to the three men standing by their chairs. "Tristan, my alpha and dearest friend. Nairn, Chief of the Farquharsons and as dear to me as a son."

"An honor to meet you, Nairn, properly this time," Tristan stated.

"An honor, Alpha," Nairn said. "Forgive us for intruding, for causing a scene, and any offense I may have caused. Wolves are nae kenned to us as a gentle lot."

"'Tis in the past, any friend of Aedan's is a friend of mine, Nairn," Tristan forgave.

Aedan turned to Weylyn. "This is my father; Weylyn."

"Aedan told me what happened with your mate, I am sorry for it," Nairn replied.

"I thank you," Weylyn replied. "But the gods smiled upon me and gifted me my with soulmate."

"'Tis glad I am. My father attempted to marry again after my mother passed but was never able to find someone he truly wanted."

"And you?" Tristan asked. "We heard you were to marry into the MacRae clan."

"Aye," Nairn sat in the chair he was offered and accepted the whisky from Weylyn. "I was, but after her brother and several of her clan were killed, we broke off the betrothal. She needed a man who was able to devote his time to being chief to her clan until her brother comes of age and no' one who already had duties."

"Anyone else on your perspective list?" Aedan asked.

Nairn chuckled and shook his head. "Nay, *father*," he teased.

Aedan laughed and raised his cup toward him. "Aye, I deserve that."

"Weylyn! Tristan!" Alexina's shrill scream came from the top of the stairs. The wolves jumped to their feet and raced up the steps, Nairn following but at a slower pace of a human. Weylyn and Tristan burst into Alexina's solar to see the women standing together, staring in horror as Eithne approached Diarmad who held baby Kyna with a knife to her chest.

"Brother!" Nairn gasped. "What are you doing?"

Diarmad looked over at his brother, his eyes wide with fear. He shook his head emphatically. "I donnae ken, Nairn please help me. I cannae stop. I am nae in control of my own body."

"Eithne, nay, stay back," Weylyn yelled.

"Give me my child, you brute," Eithne demanded.

"Please stay back," He pleaded and took a step back toward the window, the knife extended toward Eithne. "I cannae control my actions. I donnae ken what will happen."

"Where is Aileas?" Nairn demanded. Diarmad looked over at him, fear and sadness in his eyes as shook his head. Only then did they see the blood already on the jeweled dagger.

"Lucien's Dagger," Aedan breathed. "But how?"

"I need my son," Lucien said, his eyes glanced to his wife and she nodded. Bowdyn left the room to find Dagda.

"Please, whoever is controlling me, sees through my eyes. Whatever you are planning, donnae let me see or hear,"

Diarmad explained.

"Can you close your eyes?" Tristan asked. He shook his head. "Do you ken who did this to you?" Again, he shook his head.

"What happened? What do you remember?" Lucien asked.

"I was dreaming. I dreamt of a woman, beautiful beyond belief. She spoke softly to me and gave me the dagger. She told me no' to let anyone stop me. Aileas... she tried to and I..." he broke off as tears gathered in his eyes.

"Why Kyna? Why my child?" Eithne demanded. Bowdyn, Dagda, and Agora rushed in. Dagda without his tunic, but clear eyed, took in the scene around him.

"I donnae ken," Diarmad answered. "Please, forgive me! I never wanted to do this. I never..."

"We understand," Aedan said.

"Son," Lucien began. "Read my mind and assist me."

"Aye," Dagda agreed. "Whenever you are ready, da'."

"Whatever you are going to do," he began. "Do it now!" He raised the knife. Eithne screamed. Weylyn rushed forward to grab his child, and Aedan, Alexina, Tristan, Myrna, Isla, Labhaoise, Bowdyn, and Agora tried to move in on Diarmad but in that moment, everything stopped. Diarmad held the knife with a shaking hand, his arm straining with the pressure he exerted. But what caught their attention was not Dagda and Lucien, but baby Kyna.

She had one hand on Diarmad's arm holding her and her other, little palm outstretched to the knife. Her eyes glowed and flames sparked in the depths.

The infant turned to look at her father and gave an infant smile. Weylyn cautiously stepped toward her and reached out to her, as if asking if it was all right. She cooed and he grabbed her quickly, holding her to his chest and turning away from the knife.

As soon as Kyna was safe in her father's arms, Diarmad let out a shuddering breath and went lax. Aedan grabbed the knife from his hands and Tristan and Nairn held his arms.

"I am so sorry," Diarmad cried, looking at his brother. "I have never experienced anything like that before."

"What happened?" Nairn demanded, seeing Weylyn and Eithne checking their daughter.

"Is she hurt?" Diarmad begged.

"Nay, she is fine," Weylyn said but, Eithne walked over to Diarmad and slapped him.

"Touch my daughter again and you die," she stated.

"I am truly sorry, mistress. I never meant to hurt her!" He pleaded.

"What in the bloody hell is going on?" Caylean and Giorsal ran in.

"Where were you?" Dagda asked.

"Locked in my room. I could nae get out. What happened?" he demanded.

"Biróg just possessed Diarmad and tried to kill Kyna," Lucien explained.

"And if what Diarmad said is true, we have a sister to consecrate," Isla said. Diarmad looked down as Nairn placed a hand on his brother's shoulder.

"I never wanted to hurt..." he broke off as emotion closed his throat.

"It was nae you, brother," Nairn said gently.

"Then who?" he demanded.

"A Fae," Lucien replied. "A woman who has a personal issue with me."

"But how did he get the dagger?" Weylyn asked. "I

thought it killed her."

"My dagger cannot kill a Fae," Lucien replied, holding his hand out for the piece of steel. Aedan handed it to him. "It only banished her to the otherworld for one hundred years taking the dagger along with her."

"One hundred years?" Weylyn questioned. "Then my family will have to deal with her again at that time?" He held Kyna, sleeping, tighter against his chest.

"When I was there the last time, I pled our case to *the Dagda*, the All-Father, after whom you were named," he glanced at his son. "He will be sure to speak with her."

"Little good that did here and for Aileas? She is dead because of her," Eithne challenged.

"'Tis not our place to challenge the gods," Lucien said.

"'Tis, when my child is threatened," Eithne said, one hand on Weylyn's arm and the other softly rubbing Kyna's cheek.

"I will speak to Donn again and see what is happening," Lucien said, looking over at his son.

"I will try to contact Lug, he has the closest relationship with her," Dagda said. "Then place a protective hedge around Kyna."

"Place the hedge, by all means, but if you contact Lug you will mark yourself again," Lucien said.

Dagda shrugged. "I have missed my old markings. It would be of no consequence to have them again," he looked down at his mate. Agora smiled up at him in encouragement.

"Very well," Lucien agreed.

"What can I do?" Caylean stepped forward.

"Have your powers returned?" Dagda asked. Caylean looked down and shook his head.

"Then, use your warrior strength and stand guard,"

Dagda placed his palm over Caylean's heart and even through his tunic, those gathered, saw the interwoven Celtic knot design glow blue then disappear.

"What was that for?" Aedan asked his son.

"'Tis so I donnae fall asleep. Added strength, should I do battle with a Fae and prevention of me being possessed," Caylean explained. "Usually a druid cannae be possessed unless willing, but since I am nae a druid… nor a wolf at this moment, I am easily susceptible."

"Should the rest of us have the same?" Tristan asked.

"Perhaps only Alexina and you two," he turned to Nairn and Diarmad. "Fae would never inhabit wolf kind, but humans are easily manipulated."

"Then please," Alexina stepped forward. "I am willing. I would never wish to harm anyone."

Caylean looked down. "I am sorry, Alexina but I am unable to perform spells at this time."

"I can do it, son," Isla offered. Caylean nodded but took his position outside the room, standing guard.

Weylyn and Eithne carried Kyna to their room and shut the door. Dagda followed and placed a hedge of protection around their door, preventing anything from getting inside.

Chapter Five

That next morning, no one spoke about the night before. Dagda and Lucien had not returned from the stones and the women had quietly buried Aileas. When they found her, with her throat cut by Lucien's Dagger in Diarmad's room, Diarmad was inconsolable and kept to Nairn's room for the day.

After the mating ceremonies the day before, Tristan had the servants sleep-in so they would have a chance to rest and then clean up from the night before. Alexina had left their bed just after dawn to attend her duties as Lady of the Keep and Alpha Queen. Tristan knew he would find her washing dishes alongside the young lads of the pack or airing out the Great Hall, opening the shut windows. It gave him time to write a missive to Gregor Sutherland, his brother-by-mating, husband to

Tristan's half-sister Loezia and a great warrior chief. He also claimed the distinction of being wolf and Druid. He had come to their aid when Eion had attacked the keep only a month ago.

Gregor –

> *I hope Loezia and the babe are well. You have always been kind enough to lend your counsel and I find I am in desperate need of it. As chief and Alpha, only you understand the tough decision that lies before me.*

He continued his missive, explaining Aedan's connection to Nairn and what happened the night before. The memory of little Kyna's eyes burning with fire made him pause. He knew when he married Alexina, things would be different, but when Druids were introduced and they became immortal, Tristan hated to admit it, but it created a race of creatures he never knew could exist. How was he supposed to lead when he did not know the beings he led?

Huffing a sigh, he tapped his writing implement on the parchment as his eyes finally focused on what he had been staring at for a length of time.

Through his window, storm clouds gathered on the horizon and Lucien and Dagda were, making their way down the steep hill coming back to the keep.

"You have been staring hard at the incoming storm, Alpha," Weylyn's voice came from the doorway.

"The incoming storm," Tristan repeated, not turning. "Why do I feel that is an apt description?"

"Something preys on your mind, Tristan," Weylyn surmised, pushing off the doorway and walking fully into the room. "I ken I am nae Alpha, but I can listen. It has been a long time since we sat together."

"We both have been swept away with our lives and

families," Tristan agreed.

Weylyn placed a hand on his alpha's shoulder and gave it a gentle squeeze. "You will always be part of my family."

"As you will be part of mine. You raised me, Weylyn. You taught me what it is to love and be loved. You gave me the love of a father when my own would rather have seen me dead. For that, I will always be thankful."

"You have and always will be like a son to me, Tristan."

"But I am no' your son. I am Alpha and as Alpha there are things, I have to do that are no' always pleasant," Tristan said.

"Such as?" Tristan heard the hesitation in his friend's voice.

"Such as..." Tristan began. "Figuring out what your daughter is and what to do."

Weylyn let out a shuddering breath. "Tristan, I beg you. Donnae hurt her."

The pang of grief and fear hit him squarely in the chest. "I am sorry, my friend. I cannae promise that. She could be a threat to us all."

"So too, could Caylean but he learned to control it," Weylyn tried to reason. "So too, could Blane for all we ken. So too, could Bowdyn and Labhaoise and Dagda and Gregor for that matter. Kyna is a pup, an innocent wee lass. You cannae hurt her."

"I donnae want to, Weylyn but I have to ken what I am dealing with."

"I will stop you if you try," Weylyn stated, pulling himself up to his full height.

"That is nae my desire, my friend. I swear to you, please understand, my main reason for existing is to lead my pack."

"You hurt my daughter, I will nae longer be part of your pack," Weylyn threatened.

"I ken," Tristan nodded. "So that is why I donnae ken what to do."

"Please Tristan," Weylyn begged.

He closed his eyes hearing his dearest friend's plea.

"Weylyn, I donnae want to hurt any, especially no' you," Tristan started. "We donnae ken what she is. Can you swear to me on all you hold dear, she is nae a threat? Nay, you cannae, because you donnae ken. What if Biróg is within her?"

"What if she is pure and the one to save us all?" Weylyn positioned. Tristan paused and looked at him. "The world is changing, soon we will be extinct. Soon humans will rule all. Do you have a strategy for *when* that will happen? It breaks my heart to ken you would even consider it. Have I no' always been there for you? Have I no' done anything and everything for you? Have I no' given you everything? Without a word of regret? And this is how you repay me? This? I would have hoped I meant more to you."

"You do," Tristan stood and walked over to him. Weylyn took a step back. "What would you do in my place, Weylyn? Tell me."

"I would protect my pack. *All* in my pack. Nae matter what or who they are. I would garner information before I would make a decision and I would take into consideration everything my pack has done for me. If needed, I would reach out to another leader to give me some advice. I would no' hurt those I claim to love."

Tristan paused for a moment, then turned to the desk and picked up the missive he was writing and handed it to Weylyn. Weylyn read the letter but paused on the line Tristan hoped he would read with his heart, not his head.

Kyna is Weylyn's newest pup and as much as what she is worries me, she is my dearest friend's child. How do I tell him how much he means to me? How do I tell him, without him, I would nae exist? But what is his pup? Is she a threat? I cannae believe someone so innocent could mean us harm. She is like a sister to me and after everything Weylyn has done and gone through, I could nae harm him. What do I do, Gregor? I need your council.

Weylyn looked up at Tristan, tears gathering in his eyes.

"I could never hurt you my friend, for it would be like hurting myself. Please understand, I donnae ken what she is. For I want to be prepared in case someone or something comes after her." Tristan grasped Weylyn's upper arm and held his gaze.

"Who could come for her?" Weylyn asked.

"That is what I need to find out. Now, I must send this, then talk to Blane and find Lucien and Dagda. Are you... are *we* all right?"

Weylyn looked deeply into Tristan's eyes and nodded. "I donnae envy your position as Alpha, Tristan, but even though you are my leader, you are still my friend, the son I thought I never had. I will protect everyone I love and that includes you."

"Forgive me for making you believe I would ever hurt your child, Weylyn," Tristan began. "I..."

A knock at Tristan's door made them both turn. Aedan stood behind them, a wary look on his face. "Dagda and Lucien need to see you, quickly, Tristan," he said.

"Where are they?"

"Your solar," Aedan replied. "Isla is on her way up. They asked to speak with her as well."

With one last look at Weylyn, Tristan left the room.

Aedan stared at his father. "What happened?"

"How much did you hear?"

"A lot," he admitted. "Was he going to hurt Kyna?"

"He is afraid," Weylyn said. "I donnae want to believe it, but I did until he explained. He was never going to hurt her, but he believes others may and if he does nae ken what she is and how to protect her, it would be as if he was the one who hurt her. He wrote to Gregor to see if he ever experienced anything like this. He would never hurt her, but he believes I would blame him if he could nae stop them."

"I understand that," Aedan replied. "But we will always protect my sister."

Weylyn let those words sink in and he smiled. Before he lost himself in his thoughts of his daughter, he asked his son what Dagda and Lucien had said to him.

"Nothing," he answered. "Just that they wanted to see Tristan and thought it would be good to have Isla there."

"Interesting," Weylyn said. "Let us go to Blane. I ken he is worried about having revealed the pack."

"I was thinking the same," Aedan replied. "He is in his room."

Chapter Six

"What do you mean, they did nae answer you?" Tristan demanded from Dagda and Lucien. "Where are they?"

"That is what we are afraid of," Dagda replied. "I have never known the gods to not be in *Tír na nÓg*. Have you, Isla?"

"Never," she answered. "They were always supposed to be there for situations such as this, no' that these situations happen often. Lucien, of all of us you are the most powerful—"

"Oldest, I think you mean, sister," he supplied in an almost tease. "But you are right, I have never known the gods to be absent or indeed silent."

"What do we do?" Tristan asked.

"I would like to observe the new pup," Lucien stated. "I have met several hybrids. My own son is one, but never have I met one so young and in such control of her powers."

"Hybrids?" Tristan questioned. "Tell me, how is she different from Caylean?"

"Caylean, Kyna and all of the children born to a wolf and a Druid are known as hybrids. A wolf and human are known as half-breeds. Caylean was as powerful as he was, due to Isla's High Priestess blood and Aedan's undiluted first phase, as well as being conceived under the Hunter's Moon. Kyna... well, I donnae ken what she is, but all hybrids are unique in their own special way. If I could watch her, perhaps even read her thoughts, I may be able to understand her."

"How is it that only two of the many pups born to my Beta and War Chief, only those two exhibit signs of being... different?" Tristan asked delicately.

"*That* is one of life's many mysteries and even I donnae ken the answer," Lucien stated.

"The sooner we can learn what she is, the sooner we will be able to understand why Biróg wants her," Dagda said softly. The other three looked over at him. "Forgive me, da' but I seem to remember many years ago when you were teaching Striken about what he is, you said there was a time when the gods traded lives. One life for another. Could this have anything to do with bringing me back?"

Lucien stared at his son for a long moment, then took a deep breath and turned to look out the window.

"If that is true, then I worry. If the gods have chosen Kyna as their replacement due to her powers... we have much more to worry about than them not answering."

"What do you mean?" Tristan asked.

"They are coming for her and they may already be on this earthly plane," Lucien explained.

"Then we fight," Tristan stated. "I will nae allow my

friend to lose someone else."

"There is only one way," Dagda said.

"And that is?" Tristan demanded.

"Give them someone else more powerful," Dagda answered.

"We will not give either of you," Lucien replied turning from the window. "You just started your life with Agora, Kyna's life just started. We will fight or we will reason with them."

"There is nae reasoning with the gods," Isla provided.

"Gods or nae, I have seen them all bleed," Lucien said.

Weylyn and Aedan knocked on Blane's door. Odara, Blane's mate, called out, "who is it?"

"Weylyn and Aedan," Aedan replied. The door opened and Odara stood before them, her light brown hair hanging loosely around her shoulders, her dark eyes assessing. Blane sat on the bed, wearing only his trousers. He stood when he saw them.

"Weylyn, Aedan, I am so sorry. I did nae mean to cause a scene last evening," he said.

They raised their hands in peace. "Everything is all right, Blane. It was nae deliberate, you did nae ken we had guests."

"We wanted to come see you too," Aedan went on. "How are you?"

"Well, apart from worrying I exposed the pack, and wondering how the alpha will fix my mistake, we are well," Blane explained. "I must have been on the other side of the keep. I did nae spell humans near us at all. How did they get inside?"

"We are uncertain. They requested sanctuary. Tristan gave it. He is very good at channeling his father when needed," Weylyn explained. "Odara can attest to seeing and hearing how he covered."

"Indeed," the female said. "He covered quite well under the circumstances. We thank you for coming to check on us."

"Who are they? What are they doing here?" Blane asked.

"They are Highlanders," Aedan explained. "In fact, they are from my old clan, when I thought I was human."

"Did they ken you?" Blane asked.

"They do. At least the leader does. We have much to tell you, my friend. And I am sure you are nearly out of your mind being cooped up here. Come, eat with us, and we will tell you all that happened last evening. Then perhaps we can spar together? Nothing like exercise to free the body and mind."

"With pleasure, Aedan but are you sure all is well?"

"Absolutely," Weylyn promised. "Tristan is in council with Dagda and Lucien."

"Let me introduce you to my friend Nairn. He is nae a threat to us," Aedan said. "He is like a son to me."

"Gladly," he answered, accepting Odara's help in pulling on his tunic. "All is well?"

"All is... well, no' quite well, but we will talk later," Weylyn said. "I need to check on Kyna and my mate."

"I will come with you if that is acceptable," Odara offered.

"Aye, of course," Weylyn answered. "Have you broken your fast?"

"Aye, we had some porridge and fruit brought up," Blane said. "I was nae sure if I could go down to the Great Hall."

"Always, you are part of our pack. An important part. Both of you. We have much to tell you," Tristan's voice came from behind. They had sensed their alpha and caught his scent earlier and they turned to see Tristan and Isla outside the door.

"What news?" Weylyn asked. "Did Dagda and Lucien contact the gods?"

"Nay," Tristan replied.

"What do you mean, nay?" Aedan's eyes went from Tristan to his mate then back. "What has happened?"

"Come down, let us tell you over a mug of ale, I could use one," Tristan said.

Chapter Seven

Blane stood at the front gates of Sutherland Keep waiting until the chief was informed of his presence. Tristan's words rang in his ears from when they sat in the Great Hall drinking a mug of ale. *If we fail and the gods come to our plane, we may lose no' only our pack, but our world as we ken it.* Unsure of what he meant; Blane finally asked the question he had long since realized. Were the wolves around him immortal? The answer, though it surprised him they admitted it, did not shock him. But what united them all, was worry over the future of their pack. Little Kyna deserved to live and learn what she was. If the gods demanded her as a sacrifice for allowing Dagda to return to life, he would fight with all the strength within him not to allow that to happen.

The imposing figure of Gregor Sutherland appeared in the doorway of the keep. His dark brown hair still fell in short cuts at the base of his neck and his light blue eyes assessed Blane as only an alpha and leader could. He wore a tunic and leggings with his clan's colors in a sash across his chest, held in place with a Celtic brooch. Blane bowed to the leader when he reached the gate. When he raised his eyes to him, Gregor spoke.

"Tristan sent you with a missive," he stated. "My guard tells me you are part of his pack."

"I am, Alpha," Blane replied. "We fought together against Eion and the druids."

"I am Chief when in human form," Gregor answered.

"My apologies," Blane bowed again. "Chief, I am part of the pack."

"Then tell me one thing about them only someone in their confidence would ken," he challenged.

Blane took a deep breath, then squared his shoulders and looked the chief straight in the eyes. "They are immortals."

Gregor nodded slowly. "As am I," he answered. "Give me the missive."

Blane removed the scroll from the pocket Odara had sewn into the inside of his tunic. Gregor broke the seal and read silently. His brow twitched and his lips pressed together. He said nothing as he read the three pages then, once finished he sighed.

"My mate has just given me my heir two moon cycles ago, but Tristan is my brother-by-mating. Come inside, we will eat together as my men prepare to journey," Gregor offered.

"Thank you," Blane accepted. "But I was told to ask you to hurry. We donnae ken when the gods will come to our plane."

"It is but a day's journey, we will be there by nightfall tomorrow," Gregor promised. "Come, dine with us. My mate will want to hear what is going on with her family."

"Does she ken?" Blane asked.

"Which part? That her brother and uncle are immortal or that it was her other brother who tried to kill them and overtake the pack?"

Blane took a step back. "Both?"

"She kens about her brother's betrayal and I am sure she has figured out there is something unique about them," he explained.

"I will keep the confidence," he answered.

"Then come in and let us speak more of this," Gregor stated, leading him into the keep.

Striken prowled through the underbrush of the forest, near his parent's cottage. When Delia felt Biróg's defeat, she lifted the wards and Rhydian allowed him a little more freedom. He stalked a deer, focusing on his senses without phasing. His uncle Dagda trained him several years ago to be able to track without his eyes and only use his wolf sense of smell and a sixth sense he did not name but told him he would know the feeling when he felt it. Striken had never felt anything out of the ordinary until a soft breeze drifted across his skin and with it a scent he did not recognize. He froze and took a deep, silent breath, trying to harness the scent. The hair on the back of his neck stood on end and a feeling spread in the pit of his belly. The scent was not one of man, druid, or wolf, but something entirely different and he was in front of it.

Eyes wide, he turned and stumbled backward when he saw the entity stood directly behind him. Striken's heel caught a root sticking out of the ground and he fell over a fallen log. Leaning up on his elbows, he tried to muster enough willpower to phase, but the man, as he could now clearly see the shadow of a grey and brown beard covering the lower half of his face, held up his hand.

"Be at ease, Striken," the man said, his deep voice powerful. "I am no threat to you."

"Who are you? What do you want?" Striken demanded, cursing his shaky voice.

The man stared at him for a little while, his eyes hidden behind the shadow of the hooded cloak he wore. The man was tall but not as tall as Rhydian, Striken's father. He wore a dark gray over cloak that reached the tops of his leather boots, a faded blue tunic, and brown trousers. The over cloak fell around him, showing the clear outline of a broadsword at his hip which complimented the bow and quiver, full of arrows, strapped to his back.

"You have grown since last I saw you," the man said softly.

"Do I know you?" Striken studied the man, nothing about him looked familiar.

The man smiled slightly but shook his head, "alas," he said, "you would not remember me, you were but a babe when I was last in these parts."

"What are you?" he asked, suddenly curious about the scent he could not place.

"A traveler, a wanderer. No one of import, lad," he said. "But I have a message for your uncle."

"I have no uncle," the practiced response fell from his lips. No one knew of his family's connection with Dagda nor Lucien.

"You lie well," the man said. "But I do have a message for him. You must get it to him as soon as possible. His very life may depend on it." Striken tried to stop his scoff but it came out anyway. "You may not believe me, but 'tis true."

"Why do you not deliver it then, if you know who you he is? Why do you ask me to?"

"Because I am needed elsewhere," the man answered.

"Where?"

"Listen to me," the man's tone betrayed his

exasperation. "Tell Dagda, they are here. There is no time. They will meet him at the stones on the hill nearest the wolf village. Tell him. Tell him soon."

With that, the man stepped backward and before Striken could yell for him to wait, he disappeared into the fog.

Chapter Eight

Rhydian held his mate close to him as they lay together on their bed, enjoying the last vestiges of their passion while their son was away from the cottage. Delia stroked the fine hairs on his chest, as his fingers caressed the milky smooth skin of her back.

"I have missed you," Delia spoke low, her lips ghosting over his shoulder.

Kissing her hair, he tightened his grip on her. "It has been too long, my love. I am sorry."

"You should be," she teased, leaning up on her elbow giving him a chance to see her luscious curves. "It was more difficult than I imagined, seducing my mate."

Rhydian chuckled. "Aye, and I have no one but myself to blame."

"And why are you immune to my charms, husband?" she asked.

"Immune, my love? Never," he replied.

"Then what?"

"It was simply, we had far too much on our minds and of course, our son has not left the cottage. We have not been alone, and you cannot keep quiet."

"That is of your own doing husband," she teased.

"Aye, I know it," he kissed her, moving to hover over her, stroking her blonde hair out of her face. "Do you recall when your father found us in the woods, after we had pledged ourselves to each other and had yet to tell your parents?"

"Aye, and I remember how my father nearly killed you."

"It was well worth the beating I received to be able to claim you as my own."

"You could hardly keep your hands to yourself after my father blessed our union, and yet you have hardly touched me these last few moon cycles."

"Believe me when I say, I will not let it happen again. We will have to have our time alone at least once a week."

"Every week? And what if I am not agreeable?"

"I will convince you," he grinned, kissing his way from her neck to her breasts. But in a moment, he stopped and tilted his head toward their door. Delia froze and whispered to her mate.

"You felt it too?"

"Aye," he answered. "Striken." He quickly left the bed and pulled on his trousers and tunic, Delia grabbed her dress and followed her husband out of their room to the front door, which opened, and their son walked in in a daze.

"Striken?" Delia questioned.

"Son, what has happened?" Rhydian demanded. Striken looked uninjured but he was walking slowly and did not look at them.

"Something happened," he finally muttered. "We must find Uncle Dagda and Grandfather. They must be warned."

"Warned?" Delia asked, putting the kettle to boil over the fire.

"Tell us what happened, son," Rhydian led him to the chair by the fire and helped him sit.

"I honestly do not know," Striken admitted and then proceeded to tell them what happened and who he met.

"You never sensed him before?" Delia asked.

"Never," he shook his head. "But he said we have met before, saying I was very young."

"I do not know who it would have been," Delia replied. "But perhaps, someone who blessed your birth. We should contact my brother. Perhaps he knows."

"Forgive me for disagreeing with you, my love," Rhydian said. "We should go to him. It would be easier to tell him in person."

"You are right," Delia answered. "Striken, can you remember everything you just told us and tell your uncle when we see him?"

Her son nodded. "I will never forget it."

"Good," Rhydian replied. "Let us pack and go as quickly as we can. Something tells me this wanderer's message is urgent."

"Pack and we will leave as soon as we can," Delia told them.

"Mama," Striken stopped her. "Will everything be all right?"

Both Delia and Rhydian looked at each other. She then reached for her son and took his hands in hers. "What do you feel, dearest? Use your intuition."

"I am not sure," he admitted.

"What do you feel from me?" she asked.

"Hope," he replied.

"That is correct," she smiled. "Now, we must hurry. Your uncle needs us, and we cannot delay."

Striken nodded and left the room to pack, but he did not miss the subtle look between his parents, and it concerned him more than words could say.

Chapter Nine

Lucien knocked on Eithne's and Weylyn's bed chamber door. Weylyn opened the door and stepped aside. Walking in, Lucien scanned the room to see Eithne, holding her baby in the chair by the fireplace. Little Kyna looked over to see who walked in. Lucien smiled slightly and then turned to Weylyn.

"You know why I am here," he stated.

"You want to see if you can read her mind," Weylyn replied. "Isla mentioned it."

Eithne moved Kyna in her arms so the little pup could see him.

"Hello, little one. I want to read your mind. I will not hurt you," Lucien said.

I ken, he heard a foreign voice in his head.

Kyna? You can communicate with me? He questioned.

I can. You are the one they call Lucien, are you no'?

I am.

You are the oldest one.

I am.

Tell me, why do they want you?

Me? He questioned.

I hear things when I sleep. Evil people saying things. They want you. They say it is time. But they donnae say why you are evil to them. I think you are good, Kyna said.

Do you know who you hear?

Someone speaking to a man who looks like he is important. I donnae ken their names.

What have they said? Lucien asked.

They said the oldest one's time is nigh. They want him, but they also fear me. Why do they fear me? Am I bad? Kyna questioned.

Nay, little one, ancient things always fear what they have never handled before.

My grandparents have tried to help me. I hear them sometimes. My grandmother sings to me. She has such a pretty voice.

What does she sing to you? Lucien asked.

'Tis a sad song about two people who were no' allowed to be together. She cries a little every time she sings it to me, Kyna explained.

Where do you see her? Is she here?

Nay, she comes to me when I am sleeping. She smiles

when my father comes in to check on me, but tears gather when she sees my mother. Why does she cry when she sees my mama? My mama is wonderful.

I do not know, sweet one. What is her name?

She did nae tell me. She only said she was my grandmother. But she and another man are always so happy to see me. 'Tis almost as if they cannae be together without me dreaming.

Can you sleep and dream about them now? Let me see them? Lucien asked.

Can I do that?

Possibly. Hold my finger as you sleep and keep your mind open.

I will try, Kyna promised. *But tell me, why did that woman want to hurt me?*

What woman?

The one with the knife.

That was a man.

Nay, it was no'. The man was only the shell. It was a woman. She tried to hurt my mama, too before I was born. But my grandmother showed me how to defeat her. My father looked proud of me. Was he proud of me?

Aye, he was, very, Lucien smiled.

Her eyes lighted and if she was able to smile, she would have. *I like them as my father and mother. They are kind and loving. But I will try to sleep now. Can you tell my parents I love them? I cannae yet.*

I will.

Promise?

Promise. Sleep and think of our grandparents.

She nodded and closed her eyes. Her mind went blank

and Lucien felt the peace of sleep descend over Kyna. But soon her little mind opened, and a woman held her in the darkness, singing to her. Lucien pushed through the darkness and projected his image to her. The woman gasped and came fully into his line of sight. Her red hair was so bright it was unearthly, but what clenched who she was, was the pointed ears peeking out on the side of her head and the green vine markings on her pale white skin.

When his eyes met hers, the light green orbs glowed with surprise. Slowly setting Kyna down in a crib that appeared in the darkness, she stood in front of her, protectively. Her green eyes turned fiery red and flames sparked in their depths.

"Who are you? What do you want?" She demanded; her voice of the ancient Irish language Lucien had not heard in centuries.

"I am not a threat. Kyna has opened her mind to me, allowing me to see you and you to see me. It is an honor, Fae."

"What are you doing here?" She demanded, still on her guard.

"We have much to discuss. But first... where is your lover?"

"My lover?" she spat. "You forget yourself, Half Breed."

"According to the wee lass, you cry whenever her mother enters the room and you have told her to call you *grandmother.* The gods are coming after Eithne and her family. It would be best to tell me everything."

The woman stared into his eyes but finally nodded.

"Who are you?" Lucien asked.

"It appears you already know who I am," she said not dropping his gaze. "Who are you?"

"Lucien."

Her eyes widened. "*You* are Lucien?"

"I see you know of me."

"Aye," she answered. "I have been told. What are you doing here?"

"My kin are threatened."

"As is mine," she looked back at Kyna asleep in the small crib behind her.

"Tell me, is it because she is Fae, the gods want her?"

"Nay," she answered. "My grandfather has had his revenge on me. He wants... someone else."

"Your lover."

"My husband."

"Who is he? And your grandfather?"

"Selina?" another voice came from the darkness. Lucien peered, but could not see the man.

"Nay, stay back," she called to him.

"Eithne's father, I presume?" Lucien asked.

The man stepped into the light. His dark grey over cloak hid his face but Lucien sensed something familiar about him.

"Nay, my love, stay back," the Fae said again.

"It is time, Selina," he stated.

"Do I know you?" Lucien asked, the voice like a distant memory.

"Aye, you do," the man stepped further into the light and lowered the hood of his cloak. Lucien stared at him; eyes wide. "It is time, Lucien. I will tell you all. I am in the woods just outside the Wolf Village. I need to speak with all inside."

"My love?" Selina asked. He walked to her and held her to him.

"We must tell all, my love. Only then will our daughter and granddaughter be safe." He looked at Lucien. "I asked Striken to get a message to Dagda, not knowing where he was."

"He is here with me."

The man's brow furrowed. "I did not sense him."

"He is different. He has been reborn."

"Then that is the gift the gods spoke of. Come to me quickly, Lucien. There is no time and much to tell."

"I go now," Lucien agreed, still reeling from the knowledge of who Eithne's father was. Clearly Eithne was half-Fae but how had none of them known? And how had Eithne not known? So many questions swirling in his mind, Lucien broke his connection with Kyna and with a deep breath, looked up at Eithne and Weylyn. Then he saw it. A face from long ago and all began to clear.

"Did you find out anything?" Weylyn asked.

"Aye, but there is someone I must speak with and he is outside."

"Who?" Eithne questioned.

Lucien looked away from her prying eyes, eyes just like her father's.

"I must ask you to stay here. Both of you."

"If you are to meet someone who kens something about my daughter, the answer is nay. We come with you," Weylyn stated.

No time to argue, Lucien sighed and left the room, Weylyn and Eithne close behind. Odara stayed with Kyna.

Weylyn and Eithne followed Lucien as he hurried to the front gate. Looking up, Blane stood on the battlements with Bowdyn, staring down at someone on the other side of the wall.

"Open the gate!" Lucien called.

Blane shook his head. "You are nae in charge here, Druid. My alpha has been sent for and only when he agrees, will I give the order."

Lucien had no time to wait and with a flick of his wrist,

the gates opened. Blane jumped down the steps, half-phased and drew his sword. He had only just returned from Gregor's land and two of Gregor's men rallied behind him.

"Rest easy, Blane," Weylyn calmed him. "The man knows something to help my daughter."

"Even still," Blane did not lower his sword. "He is no' to enter until I hear from my alpha. He is in counsel with Gregor and on his way."

"My thanks, Blane," Tristan's voice came from behind him. "I am here now. What is going on?" They turned to see Tristan and Gregor standing side by side.

"The wanderer knows something about what Kyna is," Weylyn stated. Tristan nodded slowly.

"Lucien, do you vouch for this male?" He asked.

"Aye," Lucien turned to Tristan, the cloaked figure stepped forward.

"Then stand down, Blane," Tristan replied. "Sir, you are welcome."

The man lowered his cloak, his eyes never faltered from Eithne. Weylyn looked between them. Eithne's eyes questioned the man, but she never looked away. The wanderer took a deep breath.

"What is your name?" Tristan asked the man, but he ignored him. Walking to Eithne, he never dropped her gaze. Weylyn stepped between them.

"My alpha asked you a question, Wanderer," Weylyn said. The man finally looked at Weylyn, his light brown eyes, hollow. He said and did nothing but Weylyn felt the weight of his stare and involuntarily moved to the side. The man's eyes were back on Eithne. They stayed staring for a long moment, until Eithne took one step forward and immediately the sky darkened. The man's breathing quickened and his hand fisted.

"Do I ken you?" Eithne whispered.

The wind picked up and whipped around them.

"Aye, lass, though you would not remember," he said.

"Who are you?" she questioned.

He breathed deeply. "Eithne," he said softly. "My name is Lachlan. I am your father."

Thunder boomed and lightened streaked across the sky. Eithne's eyes grew large, then rolled back as she fainted.

Chapter Ten

The crackling of wood as it was consumed by fire and thunder's loud boom, woke Eithne. Looking around, she was in the Alpha's Solar. The large round, wooden chandelier hung high above her. Lit candles dotted the room, hardly giving light as the storm raged outside.

"Eithne?" Weylyn questioned. Beside her, her mate held her in his arms. Three figures turned from the window.

Glancing at Weylyn, she nodded. He helped her up. The men, Lucien, Tristan, and the wanderer stepped toward her.

"What happened?" she asked.

"You fainted," Weylyn explained.

"I... I was surprised," she justified.

"Nay, lass," the man said. "It was the gods. Same with this sudden storm. They do not want us together."

She finally stood and looked at the man, her gaze unwavering.

"Is it true? What you said. Are you my father?"

"Aye, I am, Eithne," the wanderer said.

"You lie, then. My parents are dead."

He looked down. "We are surrounded by wolves who can smell a lie. Ask them, am I lying?"

She looked at Weylyn who shook his head. Her brows furrowed in disagreement.

"Nay, I ken my parents are dead. I... was told."

"There is much to tell you, Eithne. But..." the wanderer stopped. "We have some little time. I will... attempt to explain."

Weylyn helped her to a bench beside the fireplace. She shivered and he sat beside her, wrapping her in his arms. She snuggled closer to him and he kissed her temple.

The man, Lachlan, accepted Tristan pouring more whisky into his cup and took a sip before he sat in front of her, on the chair Tristan usually used. The alpha waited by the shelves containing manuscripts and scrolls. Lucien leaned against Tristan's desk by the windows.

"As I said before, Eithne, I am Lachlan and I am your father. The story I am about to tell you, may seem impossible given what you know about your life, but I beg you, for the sake of Kyna, listen with an open heart and mind. I do not lie to you."

Eithne nodded and took Weylyn's hand in hers. Lachlan saw the movement and looked up at Weylyn. He smiled slightly and took a deep breath.

"Over more than a millennium ago, I was the son of a powerful druid south of here, near Antoine's Wall. I had two sisters. My father was very powerful and claimed the gods spoke only to him. I did not believe that was true. The gods are for everyone. He started... well, to be perfectly honest, to go mad. He sent me to Erin to fight in a war that was not ours. I forced him to swear he would wait to decide my sisters' fates until I returned. If he was so willing to send me to war, what would he do with them? I returned to see my youngest sister fighting him for her husband. Deena was her name. She fell in love with a Highlander, but my father wanted her with the Dark Druid of our grove." His eyes drifted to Lucien. "But... it is a long story. He banished the Highlander and killed his brother. I challenged him and became High Priest. Years past and when my sister's son, Jeeran, broke my father's curse, Deena was able to find her husband. I gave them my full blessing. It was not long after that, on a journey back from visiting my sister on the birth of their second child, I met a woman... Her name is Selina and she is Fae. Daughter of the *Tuatha Dé Danann*. Illegitimate daughter of Óengus, the god of Youth and Love, the son of *the Dagda*, the All-Father and the Nicnevin, the queen of the Fae in Alba. Selina had been trapped by her father's current lover.

"I freed her and offered to take her back to her people, but she was scared. I promised I would protect her. She journeyed to my grove where we... fell in love. We married a short time after. She was by my side for thirty years, the most wonderfully indescribable years of my existence." His face held such a far-off look, tears fell down Eithne's cheeks. He looked up at her and reached forward, wiping her tear tracks away gently. "When she told me she was carrying you... my child, my life had never felt so fulfilled. I was nearly three hundred years old then. The next morning, I woke, reached over to my wife, only to feel her side of the bed cold. I immediately got up and searched for her, but she was nowhere to be found and none of my druids knew where she was. It was as if, they never saw her. It was as if, all memory of her was gone. I searched and searched, even enlisting my other sister's husband," again he looked at Lucien. "He could not find her, but he also knew I was too tired to do much else. I had not slept for months, simply surviving on my druid powers to keep me awake. He gave me something and I fell into a deep sleep and that is where I found her. She came to me in my dreams, holding my child in her arms. She told me, her grandfather had found her and pulled her back to the *Otherworld,* punishing her for our love. No Fae was to mate with a human or druid. I swore I would find her. I will not go into how I did, but it was twenty years later. Finally, I found her, but we could not be together."

"Why?" Eithne questioned.

"Her grandfather forbade it," he explained. "I was banished back to this world with the knowledge my child would be cursed."

"Cursed?" Weylyn questioned.

"Aye, to never remember her parents nor know her true power," he said.

"But wait," Eithne shook her head. "You said this happened over a millennium ago. I am not that old. I am only one hundred and fifty."

"One hundred and forty-nine, love," Lachlan said.

"You see? I cannae be your daughter," she replied.

"There is more to the tale," Lachlan said. "Along with my banishment, I was forbidden to ever see you. But the worst part of the curse was, you would never be allowed to remember."

"Remember what?" she questioned.

"Anything," he stated. "Every one hundred and thirty years on the day of your birth, the Autumnal Equinox, at moon rise, you fall into a deep sleep for twenty years, the same amount of time I searched for you and your mother. And when you awaken, you have no memory of your previous life. I am there every time and I place you into the care of those I know will love you and keep you safe. But I am forbidden to be with you. The storm will keep getting worse the longer I stay with you. Every life you have lived, I keep trying to find a way for you to stay but every time I fail. That is a pain I carry. Every time, I see the torment on your soulmate's face as you fall into his arms. I refuse to allow you to go through that again."

"You are saying..." Eithne's voice wavered. "In one week, I will lose all memory of Weylyn, my children, my sisters and my pack?"

"If we cannot find a way to stop it... aye," he said.

Weylyn shook in her arms, his wolf close to the surface. Eithne looked over at him, his face devoid of emotion but his eyes flashed back and forth between his wolf yellow and his human as he attempted to reign in his beast.

"I refuse to lose you," she said. Weylyn turned away from her and took a deep breath. Turning back to Lachlan, she continued. "So why is Kyna so powerful and I am not?"

"You still possess your powers, but they are repressed, dormant. I am sure, if we can overcome your curse you will be able to embrace your true power. Kyna, being your first-born daughter, retains and utilizes your powers. Fae power is gifted from mother to daughter, that is why none of your sons have such."

"Eithne is the daughter of a Fae and a druid," Weylyn summarized.

"More than that," Lachlan shook his head. "She is the daughter of a Fae princess, granddaughter of *the Dagda* and my daughter. I am the oldest and most powerful of my father's line. He was the first generation of druids. Eithne's power, and by default, Kyna's power, is stronger than any living being."

No one said anything for a long moment, giving Eithne a chance to think everything through.

"If I live one hundred and fifty years and have twenty years slumber... how old am I?"

"You only are awake for one hundred and thirty years. You were twenty when you first fell, and twenty when you awaken so you may say you are one hundred and fifty, but you are only awake for one hundred and thirty years," he said. "This Equinox you will be one thousand two hundred and one years old."

Eithne's breath shuddered and she gripped Weylyn's hand tighter.

"That's..." she began. "Eight lives?"

Lachlan nodded. "As I said, your first fall was when you were twenty, so it did not count."

"Any my mate? Have I borne children?"

"The males who were your mates are dead and you never had children," Lachlan confirmed.

Weylyn looked away. Standing, he walked to the jug of whisky and poured as much as the small cup could hold, then drank it down. He was going to be sick. Feeling Eithne's eyes on him, he poured a second, then a third, and walked back to her.

"You are my one and only, Weylyn," she said.

"In this life," he replied and even he heard the bitterness in his voice. "But nae matter what, I will always be there."

Eithne shook with unshed tears but, before accepting the cup of whisky, she slid her hand around the back of his neck and pulled him closer to her.

"In every life. I feel it, Weylyn," she said, then kissed him as if it was their last kiss.

When she pulled back, Lucien spoke. "You are taking this well, Eithne."

She looked over at him. "When I was younger, when I was newly to my sisters, they told me I was a human lass who just woke from my transition into immortality. Somewhere in the back of my mind, I never believed them. Did they ken?" her gaze snapped to Lachlan.

"Only that you were a druid. I never revealed who I was to them, nor who you are. What they told you about your parent's lives was what they thought was true and when I gave you to them, I told them your grove had been decimated by Vikings while you transitioned. I only gave you up when the twenty years was nearly over. I was by your side every day."

"I would have visions, dreams, night terrors. I could never explain. Visions of me running. Part of my life seemed empty, then I met Weylyn and I felt whole again. But those dreams… they always haunted me. I kenned I was different with the Second Sight but—"

"That was your Fae power. Part of it. Fae and Druid powers alike could not be wholly suppressed. It revealed itself in your Druid abilities and your Second Sight. That is why you still have dreams and visions even after you mated. Fae women do not need to remain maidens to retain their gift."

"Where is my mother?" she asked.

"Eochaid still has her prisoner."

"For twelve hundred years?" she shrieked.

He nodded. "I have tried to help her, but I am banished."

"Why do they want Kyna?" Weylyn asked.

"She is the most powerful. They want her for them. They want her to be theirs," Lachlan said. "They will kill everyone you hold dear."

"That will nae happen," Weylyn stated.

Lachlan smiled slightly at Weylyn's vehemence. "You are the same and 'tis glad I am. I would have no one but a man worthy, for my daughter. I am happy to see you have not changed."

Weylyn looked at Lachlan questioningly. "What do you mean?" Weylyn asked.

Lachlan sighed and sat back. "They took yours, too…"

"My what?" he asked.

Lachlan leaned forward and extended his hands to Eithne and Weylyn. When they took his hand, the wind and storm outside grew in violence. Lachlan's eyes drifted to the window.

"Tell them, Lachlan," Lucien stated. "The wards will protect all within the keep."

"Very well. It is time for you to remember," Lachlan said.

"Remember what?" Eithne asked.

"Everything."

He closed his eyes, took a deep breath and a feeling akin to lightning raced through both Eithne and Weylyn. It started as flashes, but soon grew into full scenes of memory. Slowly, the picture became clearer and Eithne saw snow, woods to her left and a field to her right. Someone was pulling her through the knee-deep snow, staying close to the boundary of the woods.

"Hurry," he kept saying. "My family will help."

Her cape flowed around her as she tried to keep out the chill.

"Cinioch, wait," she called, her chest heaving with exertion. "I cannae."

"You must," he dropped her hand to turn back to her. "We are almost there."

"Nay," she threw herself into his arms. "'Tis too late." Her eyes never left the moon rising in the sky. The full white orb, so lonely in the midnight sky, until the stars around it began to twinkle. She turned to the man holding her. The Pictish markings on his face did not take away who he was. She knew that face, though it was younger and clean shaven, the face of the man she loved.

"Eithne?" he questioned.

Her soulmate.

She reached up to kiss him, a sweet innocent kiss. He held her face in his hands as he looked deeply into her eyes.

"I love you, always and forever. I will find you again," the face blurred as she fell into his arms. Her last thought was how cruel it was, seeing tears gather in his eyes.

Her Weylyn.

Another memory surfaced. She was riding a horse, a man seated behind her. A line of Roman Legionaries before them, but the horse's gallop did not slow. Before they were trampled, the Romans stepped aside and split down the middle allowing the horse and riders through. But instead of coming after them, the Romans saluted and formed ranks behind them to ward off an assault, giving them a chance to ride away. But their screams haunted her.

"Stop," she ordered.

"Nay, we must get away. I will protect you, always and forever."

"I will not have them die for me. Let me go, Caius."

He paused and, being behind her, she could not see him, but as he shifted and swung off his white horse, she felt the cool metal of the breast plate and saw the leather trousers and long red tunic. Standing beside the horse, his helmet covered most of his face. The pure look of Roman General should have worried her but when he offered his arms up to her, she slid down the horse and into his chest.

The sounds of fighting lingered behind them, but she gazed up at him. He pulled off his helmet, the Red Crest brushing her face as he lowered it. When he looked back at her, her breath caught. "I love you, Eithne, gods help me, but I do."

"I love you too," she said. The hair may have been different, but as her memories surfaced in the Alpha's Solar, she took Weylyn's hand beside her. She would know his face anywhere.

"Remember me," he begged.

She nodded as tears pricked the back of her eyes. It was always so unfair.

"Marry me, Caius," she begged. "Let me call you husband before I forget your name."

The Roman before her, lowered his head to hide his tears. "It would be my honor, Eithne."

He turned behind them and grabbed a handful of the closest flower he could find. Turning back to her, he shrugged. "Not what I would have given you, but wolf's bane always smelled sweet to me."

"They are beautiful," she took the bouquet and faced him. The love she had for him, overflowing. "What do I say in your traditions?"

Caius took her hands in his and stared into her eyes. "Do you consent, before the gods and others, to be my wife?"

"I do."

"Then say these words; *quando tu gaius, ego gaia.*"

She repeated the words and he swallowed audibly.

"I love you, Eithne and by the power of your voiced consent and the words you spoke to me, we are joined as one."

Her eyes drifted to the moon rising over his shoulder and tears spilled down her cheeks. "Then kiss me... husband."

Slowly, he moved to take her face in his hands. Their eyes remained locked as he lowered his lips to hers. The touch was warm and filled her with love but soon, she felt the *whoosh* of air behind her and she crumpled to the ground. Caius let out a cry and his tear streaked face was the last thing she saw, until the world went dark.

Scenes flashed in her mind, every one hundred and thirty years she fell in love and every one hundred and thirty years, her memories were taken from her, but one thing remained constant; Weylyn. Be it Cinioch the Pict, Caius the Roman General or any of the other faces that flashed before her, her one constant was, she always found her soulmate and as he squeezed her hand in his that day in the solar, she opened her eyes and looked over at him.

"What was that?" Weylyn breathed.

"What?" she questioned.

"Did you... see... us?" he asked.

"You saw it too?"

"Saw... and felt, as if it was my own pain. I remember."

"So do I," she answered. "Cinioch, Caius, Weylyn all the lives we lived together."

"But how?"

"The gods," Lucien stepped forward. "Anu, the Mother goddess negotiated all of her children to have a soulmate and to be given the opportunities to find them. It was her gift to you but the god who cursed you used it against you, never letting you claim your mate until it was too late... until Weylyn. You met him far earlier than all the others."

"What happened to the others? To my soulmate after I..."

"The gods show no mercy," Lachlan said.

Weylyn's hand pulsed in hers. She looked up at him. "I remember each and every one... donnae ask, my love. You donnae need that burden."

She pressed her lips together and closed her eyes. "I am sorry."

"Nay, I gladly would do it again," Weylyn pledged.

"You would not remember, Weylyn," Lucien began. "But we fought together afterward. I knew Caius well. That is why I stared at you when we first met at the entrance to the cave. I had not seen your face since he fell in battle. He was one of my dearest friends. I did not know what was happening and since you obviously did not remember me, I waited. Caius fought for his lost love and died well. Eithne was part of my grove for a time, and when he fell in love with her on one of his many visits, he turned from the Roman Conquest. When he lost her, he wanted no one to defile his memory of her and her love of Britannia. We fought to drive the Romans back behind Antoine's

Wall."

"I recall but flashes," Weylyn admitted. "But I remember when she fell, each time. I thought her dead. Why? If she merely lost her memory, could I no' have helped?"

"When Eithne loses her memory, she not only loses all memory, but she remains asleep for twenty years. None of your former lives were immortal. And the anger you felt was directed toward the gods and they showed you no mercy." They both looked back at Lachlan who tried to smile but his eyes were heavy with regret.

"Is there a way to stop this?" she begged. "I cannae leave Weylyn and my children. Is there any way?"

"The only thing we can do is speak with the gods. Reason with them," Lachlan stated.

Lucien scoffed. "Have you tried reasoning with them?"

"It is the only way," he said. "I will do all in my power to save my daughter." He turned to Weylyn. "As I know you will."

"I believe I have proven that over the millennia," Weylyn answered.

"You have indeed."

A knock on the solar door drew their attention. Tristan called for the person to enter. Aedan opened the door and took in the scene around him. Saying nothing about Eithne's tear-streaked face nor Weylyn's death-like grip on the whisky cup, he addressed his alpha and Lucien.

"Rhydian, Delia and Striken have arrived. Dagda is with them now," Aedan said.

"They came to deliver my message," Lachlan stated. "As I mentioned, I was coming to you, Lucien but I did not feel Dagda was here and we will need all warriors when we face the gods."

"Let us go and welcome my daughter's family, if that is agreeable with you, Alpha," he asked Tristan. Agreeing, Tristan turned back to Weylyn and Eithne. Lucien continued. "Lachlan has given you much to think over. I knew when I first heard of you, Eithne there was something special about you and now I know what it is. But know this, niece, you may have succumbed to the gods' curse for over a millennium, but my dear, you have us now. We will not allow them to hurt you again."

Eithne nodded and thanked him. Once she and Weylyn were alone, they stayed in silence for a time. Weylyn refilled the cup of whiskey and offered it to her. Eithne took two large sips before giving it back. Again, they were silent, apart from the crackling fire and the thunderstorm raging outside.

Soon, the soft sound of someone playing the lyre to welcome their guests to dinner filtered up. Weylyn and Eithne sat in silence, then finally, she turned to her husband and stared at his face. A face she knew well, the face she loved in every life she lived. The face she wanted more than any other. The face, in one week, she would not remember. She remembered the pull she had to him when she first laid eyes on him. Aedan carried him into their cavern in Wolf's Bane Field over thirty years ago. She remembered the overpowering need to save him and how she knew him but did not know how she knew him. Her soul cried out for him. He was her soulmate. Somewhere in the back of her mind, even then, she must have known who he was. Who they were to each other and who they would become.

Tears bubbled to the surface and streamed down her cheeks, blurring her vision. Weylyn wiped them away as they kept falling and soon, she saw the mirroring tears on his face.

"Promise me two things," she finally said, voice broken by emotion.

"Anything."

"You take care of our children and you swear you will be there when I wake to remind me how much I love you."

His body shook as his tears increased.

"I swear on everything I hold dear, should the worst happen, I will take care of them and be there by your side."

"I love you, Weylyn. You and only you as was proven in our past. I love you more than any other. And I promise if it is within my power, I will fight for us and for you," she promised.

Weylyn framed her face in his hands and kissed her. In all thirty years they had been mated, he had kissed her in every way, a simple kiss good morning, a sweet loving kiss when she carried their pups, a passionate kiss as they made love, never before had he kissed her the way he kissed her in that moment. The pure desperation in his movements, as if he could keep her with him just by willing it. She tasted their tears as they mixed together. The sounds of the fire and storm dulled as every other sense heightened.

Eithne felt him try to pull away but she refused to allow him to stop. She needed her mate, wanted to feel alive, desired to be loved by him the way only he could. Burying her hand into his hair, she kept him pressed to her. She did not pause, even when she sat up to straddle his lap. Instinctively, he understood and pulled her closer. She felt every part of him, her mate, husband, lover, soulmate.

After a moment, he slid to the floor. She was still tucked against him. Pulling back then, she allowed it and watched as he pulled his tunic over his head. She tugged at the strings holding her bodice but stopped when Weylyn's hands took over. She lay before the fire watching the heat dance in her mate's eyes.

Soon they were bared to each other, but instead of falling into their usual dance, Eithne paused. Her hand and eyes trailed up Weylyn's torso, the fine hairs on his chest, tickling her palm. She memorized every dip, every plane, every muscle and every scar. Her hand moved up to his shoulders, the broad, strong shoulders that held their children aloft. The shoulders she rubbed after a difficult day to help him relax. The shoulders that used to carry the weight of the world but had been lighter since they mated. The corded muscle that fanned from his neck. The vein on the side of his neck that pulsed when his heart beat too fast just as it did then.

The square jaw covered in a few days' worth of stubble,

his full lower lip and thinner upper lip, tinged pink with the bruising force of her kisses. The straight nose leading up to dark eyes, set under thick brown eyebrows and high forehead. He took her breath away. For a long moment they stared at each other, both memorizing the moment but as he leaned down, pressing his chest against hers, capturing her lips in another kiss, she swore she would do everything she could to stay with him.

He was her always and forever.

Chapter Eleven

The storm raged outside the keep walls as Lachlan, Lucien and Tristan followed Aedan down the stairs to the Great Hall. Dagda and Agora along with Bowdyn, Labhaoise, Isla, and Alexina stood greeting their guests. Striken's eyes grew wide as he looked up and saw Lachlan.

"Mother," he whispered. Delia looked over at her son but Striken never dropped Lachlan's gaze. "'Tis him." Delia's eyes followed her son's and locked on him.

"Uncle?" she breathed.

"'Tis good to see you, Bedelia, Rhydian," he said. The Bearman's face flashed with recognition, surprising Lachlan. He had only met the Viking shifter when he and Delia had Striken.

"Son, it is well," Delia said. "This is your uncle, Lachlan. He is my mother's brother."

"Then why did you not tell me that?" Striken demanded from him. "Why tell me you are a wanderer and frighten me?"

"Because I am a wanderer. I am sorry if I frightened you, lad," Lachlan said. "But I could not tell you who I was for fear of the gods hearing."

"Why are you a wanderer?" Tristan asked.

"When I was searching for my wife, I left my grove for too long and those that were not killed, converted to Christianity. When I returned, my grove was decimated and I was not remembered," Lachlan admitted.

"Lachlan?" A female voice questioned from the stairwell. Lachlan and Lucien turned to see Myrna staring at him. "Is it really you?"

"Aye, sister, 'tis," he answered, and a ghost of a smile lifted his lips.

Myrna hurried across the flagstone floor and into her brother's arms. "'Tis so wonderful to see you!" she exclaimed.

"And you, dear one," he answered.

"Forgive me for not telling you, my love," Lucien said. "He only just arrived, and we needed to speak with Eithne, urgently. I did not know where you were."

"I was looking after Kyna and the other children with Odara," she revealed as she embraced her daughter, Rhydian, and Striken. "But come, sit with me and tell me how you have been. Did you ever find Selina?"

Lachlan shook his head as he allowed his sister to escort him to the table.

"Let us have some music," Tristan called and one of the pack struck up his lyre. Alexina left to go to the kitchens, asking food and ale be brought out to their guests.

"I will not be able to stay long, Alpha," he said. "The

storm will grow in intensity the longer I am close to my daughter. I have no wish to bring your keep down."

"You will stay however long you desire," Tristan answered. "And we will greet you as an honored guest."

Conceding to the alpha, Lachlan sat with his sister, answering all her questions but his daughter was never far from his thoughts. He stopped praying years ago but he hoped and said a silent prayer, they would be able to save his daughter this time. He could not see the pain on her face nor sense the agony Weylyn went through every time, ever again.

Weylyn's hand stretched beside him as he lay on his stomach in his room. When all he felt was empty coverings, his eyes shot open and he sat up.

"Eithne?" he questioned. When no one answered, fear grew in the pit of his stomach and he tore at the furs that covered the bed. Yanking on his trousers, he ignored his tunic and raced to the door, throwing it open.

Her scent filled the hallway and he nearly ran down the corridor. Not wanting to wake anyone yet, he followed her scent and soon slowed when he figured out where she was. The door at the end of the corridor was cracked open and a soft light poured through the opening. Weylyn slowly padded to the door and peeked in. As expected, Eithne stood with a candle, softly stroking their youngest son's hair as silent tears rolled down her cheeks.

He was going to open the door, when he heard her voice and stopped.

"Grow strong, grow kind, grow well, my son. Listen to your father and brothers and protect your sister. I will always love you and I will always be there for you. My dear heart, forgive the pain I cause when I leave. But ken I would stay if I could." She leaned down and kissed his forehead. Closing her eyes, her tears slid off her nose and onto his skin. The young boy moaned softly and turned over in a huff. Eithne pulled back and stroked his hair. Then, she turned and looked down in the cradle to where Kyna slept. Weylyn watched as she reached down and stroked her cheek.

"Shh, hush, little one," she soothed. Weylyn could not see what Kyna was doing but Eithne reached down and kissed her forehead. "Promise me, you will grow and remember who you are and where you come from. I love you so very much, dearest. I have always wanted a daughter to watch grow and share things with. I may not be there for you but ken I will always love you. Listen to your father and brothers. Protect them, my little warrior lass. Never forget me, please."

Her voice cut off as her body shook. Weylyn opened the door and hurried to her as her knees gave out and tears and emotions broke her. Maneuvering them both out of the room and to the corridor, Weylyn shut the door just as Eithne fell into his arms and she cried harder than she ever had before. Sinking to the floor when her legs could not hold her, Weylyn held her tightly to his chest as her sobs wracked her body. His own tears wet her hair, but he said nothing.

Soon her cries subsided but the pain was still there. Weylyn helped her up and they slowly walked to their room.

Chapter Twelve

That morning, the morning of the Equinox, Weylin looked over at his mate lying beside him. They had not slept since he found her in the nursery. Not wanting to miss a moment of what could be their last night and morning together for twenty years, they stayed awake, simply holding each other and memorizing their faces. The sun was well on its way to its height but still they stayed abed.

Weylin felt the moon cycle's full moon and his wolf itched to be released to save their mate. Even though they were no longer slaves to the moon, every full moon, Weylin felt a restless energy from his wolf.

Eithne stroked his face and kissed him once more, not an invitation to be together, simply a gentle good morning kiss but he savored it as if it were the last kiss they would have.

She stood and pulled on a plaid blanket over her sleepwear. Walking to the window, she wrapped her arms around herself and stared out. Weylyn watched from the bed. He did not like the resignation in her shoulders. She had cried so many tears the night before, her eyes were dry, but the compliance he saw in her posture, forced him to stand. Weylyn left his tunic on the chair as he walked over to her. His hands came gently down on her shoulders and she leaned back into his chest.

They stood there for several minutes but to them it felt like hours. Lachlan and Lucien had scoured the archives, both in the library of the keep where Isla and Labhaoise had stored scrolls from their grove, for a cure. They even journeyed with Isla and her sister through the portal to Skye to look for answers in their father's library. Gabhran may have turned to a wolf when Marrock had bitten him but the shape shifter had kept accurate records and Isla hoped, perhaps he had figured out what Eithne was and had researched it while he was alive. But if they had found anything, they had not told them.

After nothing but peaceful silence, the strong two taps at the door made them jump. Heading to the door, he looked back at Eithne who nodded, and he opened it.

Aedan, Tristan, Caylean, Dagda, Lucien, Blane, Labhaoise and their mates, along with Gregor, stood on the other side. Weylyn locked eyes with his son who smiled slightly.

"May we come in?" Aedan asked.

Weylyn nodded and opened the door wider. Once everyone was inside, Weylyn shut the door and headed back to his mate. Wrapping his arm around her, he waited.

"We wanted to come to you today," Isla stepped forward. "To tell you how much we love you and how we will fight for you." Her eyes went up to Weylyn. "For both of you. We will not let this happen again. No' this time."

"I thank you all for coming and for being so willing to

fight for me, for us," Eithne took Weylyn's hand. "But I will nae have any of you hurt. I have made peace with it. They will nae take my daughter, that is my main concern. But I thank you. You all mean so much to me, I cannae tell you how joyous it is to ken how many friends I have. Aedan, Tristan, I have only one request of you."

"Name it, lass," Aedan swore.

Her eyes moved to Weylyn. "Be there for Weylyn. He will need you both. Please. Promise me."

Weylyn's body shook but she ignored it.

"You did nae need to ask, lass," Tristan promised. "But I swear."

"As do I," Aedan said.

"This is madness," Weylyn finally exploded.

"Weylyn."

"Nay, nay I refuse to stand around and exchange vows of love and protection when we should fight. Flee. Get away from here."

"Fight, what?" Lucien questions. "The gods?"

"Aye, better than waiting. Or flee."

"Flee, where?" Lucien challenged. "Do you not recall all the other times? It is not going to change the fact that at moon rise this evening, Eithne will lose all memory no matter where she is and there is nothing you can do about it."

Weylyn roared and flew toward Lucien. Grabbing him by his tunic, he slammed him against the wall. Ignoring everyone around him yelling his name, he leaned in and growled.

"I have had enough of your riddles, Dark One. Instead of warning us, why do you nae work to find a way to save my mate? Or perhaps you donnae ken the pain of losing her."

"You may be angry, Weylyn but you are no coward."

"Coward?" Weylyn demanded.

"Flee? Well... maybe you are, and you are finally showing it."

Weylyn let out a roar that echoed throughout the keep and half-phased, sinking his teeth into Lucien's neck. Everyone screamed but his wolf would not stop. He threw punches and tore at Lucien until he felt his life's blood on his claws and Lucien fell to the floor, dead.

Weylyn panted from the fight but soon the horror of his actions filled him. Looking down at Lucien's prone form, he phased back to his human form.

"Dear gods, what have I done?" he gasped. His eyes taking in the shocked faces around him.

"You let the wolf out. Now, perhaps we can come up with a plan without your wolf wanting to fight us all?"

Weylyn looked passed everyone to a darkened corner of the room. Lucien stepped forward. Weylyn looked down at the body at his feet, it was gone, as was the blood on his hands. He looked back at Lucien.

"A little trick I learned from an old Nordic friend," Lucien said. "I knew your wolf needed out. Now, is he contained?" Weylyn nodded. "Good, the gods are moving. They will be here soon. We need to meet them."

"Where?" Aedan asked.

"On the field just beyond the standing stones," Lucien explained.

"So near?" Tristan questioned.

"It is better there than at the gate," Lucien said. "Now, I would suggest someone stay with the children, but we will need Kyna."

"Nay," Eithne snapped. "I will nae allow my daughter anywhere near them."

"Not to give her to them but as a bargaining tool."

"Still, my answer is nay," she stated. Her sisters went up to her to give comfort. "Nay," she shook them off.

"Eithne, I swear to you, no harm will befall her," Lucien said.

"How do I trust you? You tricked my husband into revealing his wolf."

"You know you can trust me, niece," he said.

"You have called me that before. Why?"

"Because that is what you are. Your father and my wife are brother and sister. So, on our relationship, I swear, no harm will befall your daughter, but we must have her there. It will lull them into a false sense of victory."

Eventually, Eithne agreed. "Will Lachlan meet us there?" She had yet to feel comfortable in calling him *father*.

"He will," Dagda answered. "Due to the storm that happens whenever you both are together, he could not stay here, though he wanted to stay with you last evening. He will be waiting for us."

Eithne nodded slowly. "Then we must prepare. Perhaps a meal before we leave?" she asked Alexina.

"Already laid out for us," Alexina said.

"And Aedan? Could you be sure my bow and quiver are ready?"

"Of course," Aedan answered.

"The wolves will be half-phased," Tristan announced. "Rhydian will be in his bear form. All will be well, Eithne."

Looking over at Weylyn, she nodded, though the memories of the Romans who gave their lives for her and the people of the Celtic village two lives ago who stood up against the gods for her and were killed with a mere wave of *the dagda's* hand, caused a cold shiver to run up her spine. She would never forgive herself if anything happened to the wolves and druids before her. She would gladly sacrifice for them.

"Someone should stay with the children," Labhaoise said.

Odara stepped forward. "If it would be acceptable, Alpha, I will stay with them." Her eyes drifted to Eithne. "I would fight for you any day, as I consider you a sister, but," she looked over at Blane, took his hand, then placed her other on her lower abdomen. "I cannae put two lives at risk."

Eithne covered her mouth as a soft cry escaped. She rushed to her friend and embraced her as tears streamed down her cheeks. Odara had become her dearest friend and had, on more than one occasion cried to Eithne wondering if she would ever be able to give Blane the pup he so desperately wanted. "Of course, you must stay. I would never ask any to put their lives in danger for me, but especially no' one who carried the future."

"I will pray for you and I will protect them all with my life," Odara swore.

"I am pleased for you both," Tristan took Blane's arm in a warrior's shake.

"Our thanks, Alpha," Blane said. "We were going to wait to share, but it seemed appropriate."

"One thing," Caylean said. "I donnae want Giorsal there, no' in her condition."

"Excuse me, mate?" Giorsal questioned, raising an eyebrow.

"You must think of our child."

"I will be with my family," she stated, a challenge in her voice.

"Take the children to my solar," Tristan continued as if they had not spoken. "You ken the secret door, if something happens to us, take them and flee to Gregor's land. He has sent Loezia a missive asking her to stay vigilant for any travelers seeking sanctuary. She will be looking for you, if needed."

"She will be expecting you to tell her our son's name,"

Gregor prompted.

"Which is?" Odara asked.

"Dearg Faolán Sutherland," Gregor stated.

"Aye, I will remember, and do as you say, Tristan," Odara promised.

"There will be wards around the castle to be sure you are protected, Odara," Dagda stated.

"We will be fine. I thank you, Dagda," she said.

"Blane, I ask you to stay with Odara," Tristan began. When Blane tried to protest, Tristan held up a hand. "Please, you are an excellent warrior, but also, I would have our children follow nae other if the worst should happen. They will need a father."

Blane stared at his alpha but eventually nodded. *"If* that happens, I will protect them and teach them of their origins."

"I thank you," Tristan said. Then turning back to his pack, he took a deep breath. "I am nae one for long speeches before battle but ken this, I could nae have asked for a better pack nor wolves to call my friends. Nor druids to claim as family. That is something I never thought would or could happened. We go to war with the gods. We may no' survive but there is nae another I would rather have by my side, nor fight for, than you all. I love each of you and today, come victory or defeat we can claim to have fought for innocence and love. I say we fight the gods and let them all ken, we will nae allow them to take our lives, our freedom, our love. Fight for love. Fight for the future. I am honored to be your alpha, and should we be victorious today, I will always say how our pack fought for the best reason... family."

Chapter Thirteen

After breakfast, the pack began to gather their things. Aedan had sharpened all weapons during the week. They prepared to leave. Odara and Blane headed up to the nursery, and the rest walked to the main door of the keep.

"Aedan!" Nairn called from the stairs. Aedan turned back to him while all others filed out the door. "What is going on? Why do you wear battle leathers? What has happened?"

"Nairn, I cannae say much but I will tell you, if we donnae return, I need you to help Odara and Blane get our children to safety. Can you do that for me?"

"What is going on?"

"We fight."

"Then let me, us, my brother and I, fight with you," Nairn said.

"Nay 'tis nae your fight."

"It is yours and I fight for you," Nairn pledged.

"Nair, nay," Aedan replied. "There is nae a good outcome to this battle."

"Donnae do this, Aedan," he said. "I am nae the six-year-old boy you once kenned. I can fight and I will."

Aedan stared into his eyes but saw the determination. "We fight the gods."

Nairn started, "the gods? *The* gods?"

"Aye, they want to take Kyna."

Nairn's face turned hard as stone. "Is that why Diarmad was possessed by that creature? She was a god and wanted Kyna?"

"She was Fae, but aye."

"Why? What is she?"

"She is my sister… but she is powerful beyond belief. Her mother is Fae and druid. And of course, my father."

"Aye, a wolf," Nairn finished Aedan's thought. "She is an innocent wee lass."

"Aye, that is why we fight. Well, that and if we donnae, Eithne will succumb to the curse the gods have imposed upon her and forget us all."

"Including her husband and children?"

"Aye," Aedan replied.

Nairn shook his head. "Aedan, let us help. I will nae have anyone lose someone so dear."

"There is nae assurance of survival."

"Then I fight and fall by your side, brother," Nairn said,

offering his arm to Aedan.

Aedan stared at it for a long moment before nodding and accepting his warrior's shake.

"Gather weapons and Diarmad and hurry. Meet us on the field near the standing stones."

Nairn nodded once and rushed up the steps to his room to gather his weapons.

Aedan hurried out the door and caught up with his family as they crested the hill. Lachlan was already waiting for them, staring off to the horizon. Eithne held Kyna in her arms and walked to her father.

"Did you learn anything?" she asked him. He had left the night they met, to go with Lucien to research a cure for her sleeping sickness. She had not seen him since. When he did not answer, she went on, "any way of preventing this?"

Lachlan turned to his daughter and gently stroked her cheek; a soft smile tipped the corners of his lips.

"All will be well," he said. "I have let you and your mother down for over twelve hundred years, no more. Never again."

"What are you saying?"

His smile increased for a moment, then he leaned forward and kissed her forehead only pulling back when a crow caw pealed overhead. Looking up, they saw the bird circle them, then land on a tree branch. Instantly, the tree's orange leaves of Autumn, shriveled and blew away in the wind. The tree, dead.

"They are here," Lucien stated.

"What was that?" Weylyn asked.

"The crow," Dagda said. "'Tis The Morrigan. The goddess of War."

The crow squawked, eyeing the small band. Nothing happened for the longest time apart from the crow preening its feathers. But then they heard it, the rhythmic pounding of drums. It was faint but the wolf ears caught the sound.

The warriors shifted from foot to foot, the itch of battle, strong. Aedan unsheathed his two dirks and gripped them loosely. Nairn, Diarmad, and Gregor did the same. The wolves half-phased and Rhydian changed into his bear. The druids; Labhaoise, Isla, Bowdyn, Delia, Dagda, Agora, and Myrna gathered together preparing to use their communal power. Caylean and Giorsal hung back but Giorsal had her bow in hand and Caylean had an arrow already notched in his, waiting.

Suddenly, the drums stopped.

"They will want Kyna. That will never happen," Lachlan stated.

"Go, da'," Eithne finally said. "Take Kyna and go."

"Nay," he answered.

"I ken what you will do. You will give yourself over to them in exchange. You cannae." Eithne stared at him.

"I have run from this for over a century. Today, I stop running. If I had offered myself to them sooner perhaps you could have been happy with your soulmate."

"I am happy with him," she said. "And Weylyn is the one I am supposed to be with for the rest of time."

"I think so too," Lachlan said softly. Weylyn stood beside her and looked over at them, the yellow eyes of his half-phased wolf, assessing. "You may want to hide Kyna," he said. "Best they do not see her initially."

Eithne nodded and looked behind her, scanning the group to see who would take her. Isla stepped forward and offered. Grateful her sister took her, Eithne turned back to the field and slid her hand down Weylyn's arm, unable to take his hand since his claws extended from his fingers. Weylyn looked over at her and nodded.

"Thank you," she said. "Both of you," speaking to his wolf, she continued. "For being mine and standing by my side."

"Always," he answered.

A loud boom echoed around them and immediately the gods stood before them on the other side of the field.

"They are here," Lucien said on the other side of Lachlan.

For a long moment, they stood facing each other, then, without words, *the dagda* motioned for something to be brought forth. Two men pulled a chain and struggled to bring their charge forward. When they finally did, Lachlan gasped.

The fiery red hair, pale skin, green vines and eyes of his wife came into view.

"Selina?" he breathed. She looked up to him. Her eyes growing large then she turned her gaze to Eithne standing beside him.

"Nay! Flee!" she screamed, only to be hit across the face and fall to the ground.

Lachlan roared but Lucien held him back.

"'Tis a test," he said. "A trick. They want you to charge."

"Then so be it," Lachlan replied, rubbing his fingers together then snapping them, his powers sparked and glowed blue at his fingertips.

"Think of Kyna," Lucian said. Lachlan stopped immediately and looked over at his granddaughter, her brown eyes watching. He calmed slightly.

"Let me handle this," Lucian stated. Lachlan said nothing and Lucien stepped forward. "Quite the performance, Eochaid," he spoke to the All-Father. "Tell me, what do you hope to accomplish?"

"You tell me, Lucien," *the Dagda* said. "You bring a force against us. Are we not to defend ourselves?"

"We knew not why you came here," Lucien went on. "We were not sure if you came to fight or not."

"That depends," *the Dagda* stated.

"On?"

"On your willingness to stand down," he said. "Give us the child. We gave you your son's life, now we want the child. Only she is the most powerful."

"That is not a condition we are prepared to agree upon," Lucien said.

"We would gladly give our life back in exchange for hers to be spared," Dagda called.

"You are hardly as powerful," *the Dagda* stated. "And we are not in the habit of taking back what was freely given."

"It was not freely given if you demand another life for it," Lucien answered.

"The child will grow up well loved. Anu has agreed to nurture her," *the Dagda* said.

"Forgive my disbelief, Eochaid," Lucien said. "You chain your own granddaughter and keep her prisoner for over a millennium. I do not trust you will protect this child."

"Her crime is different and her punishment just," he said.

"Crime?" Lachlan spat. "What crime do you claim she committed?"

"She knew it was forbidden to mate with a human or a druid," *the Dagda* said.

"Is it not also forbidden to take another to your bed while you are married to someone else, and then hide the pregnancy?" Lucien asked.

The Dagda's eyes grew wide and his face flushed with anger. The Morrigan flew and landed as a human beside *the Dagda.* Her black hair and dark eyes assessing the men.

Lachlan went on. "You desire to take this innocent child simply because you believe she is powerful. But she is only a babe... take me."

"Or me," Lucien stepped forward even more. "I was the

one who begged you to let my son live and now these wolves, my kin are suffering for it."

"You do not understand, Lucien," the Morrigan said. "You have learned all we desire to teach you. She is a child and therefore able to absorb all of our teachings. She is more powerful than you and even your son. We want her for her abilities, aye, but more for her childlike mind."

"I have read her thoughts," Lucien revealed. "She is older than she looks. An old soul." Lucien looked over at his friend Donn, god of the Dead, then back at the All-Father. "I was told you would ask for something in return, but never did I expect something so great as a child's life. I say nay."

"We are the gods, you cannot say nay to us," *the Dagda* said.

"Even gods bleed. When I was on the battlefield with you, I fought, and I killed. And do you ken who I killed? *Tuatha Dé* as well as *Fomorians* and they both bled and died. So donnae tell me you are indestructible." They stared at Lucien for a long moment.

"Let me ask this," Lachlan said. "Kyna said the gods claim the oldest one's time is nigh. Am I who you truly want? For I will freely come with you in exchange for no threat to my granddaughter and the curse my daughter is under to be lifted for all time."

"Nay," Eithne breathed.

"Stay back, Eithne," Lachlan said. "Keep Kyna away."

Eithne looked back at Isla who held her daughter, Kyna's eyes ever watchful. She locked eyes with her mother and a strange tingling sensation began in Eithne's fingers. Turning back to the gods, she began speaking.

"You have robbed me of my mother, my father, my soulmate for the last twelve hundred years. You have stolen my life, but what you feared still surfaced. I may no' be as powerful as some but, I am stronger than most think. Your repression of my abilities failed to be as effective as you would have hoped. I am a druid. I am a Fae. And I am what you fear the most. One of you."

In that moment, Selina gathered the strength she had, and her power glowed in her hands like a fire. She expelled the power toward Eithne who had her arms outstretched, body open, waiting for the transfer from her mother.

"Eithne!" Weylyn shouted but she said nothing as the transfer was like an all-consuming fire. She gasped as the fire subsided.

"Eithne?" Weylyn questioned. The energy gave her all of her memories, powers and knowledge back. When she opened her eyes, she felt the power course through her almost like she was heady with too much wine. Looking over at Weylyn's questioning face, she nodded. Then turned back to the gods.

"No one is dying today. No one is being sacrificed and no one will forget. Now give me back my mother."

The Dagda took a step back when the flames in her hands glowed red like fire. Eithne's body changed too, her hair changed to a fiery red, green vine markings appeared on the pale skin of her right arm and her ears became pointed. Her eyes glowed red as flames swirled in the depths. Lug drew back beside *the Dagda* aiming the golden spear at her.

Weylyn phased into his full wolf, standing on all fours, just as the spear was loosed. He jumped into the air and caught the spear in his teeth. He landed at Eithne's side, crushing it to pieces with one strong clamp of his jaw. He growled as he took a protective stance beside his soulmate.

"Are you unable to hear, All-Father?" Eithne mocked. "I said, give me back my mother."

The men holding the chain dropped it and took a step back. Oengus, Selina's father, rushed to his daughter and held her up. Tearing off the iron collar around her neck, he framed her face with his hands.

"Forgive me, daughter," he said. "I did not know they kept you prisoner. They said you had your mate. I did not know." His eyes searched her face, but she nodded slightly. Oengus' eyes turned to fire like Selina's had in Kyna's dream and Eithne's were currently. He snapped them toward his father. "Go now, go my sweet one. I always loved you."

Selina took her chance and hobbled to her feet. Lachlan looked at Eithne who nodded, and he rushed forward to his wife. They met halfway on the field. She fell into him and he lifted her, cradling her in his arms. There was no time for sweet words between them. Lachlan raced back to the group.

Once they were safe, Eithne addressed the gods again. "You will forever be nothing more than legend, myth and whispers of a once great nation," she cursed. "Remember who I am for I shall not remember you. Now. Be. Gone." Oengus pulled out his dagger and wrapped his arm around his father's neck, the dagger at his throat.

"We have things to discuss, Father," he spat. *The Dagda* smirked but with a snap of his fingers, Oegnus' arm snapped and the bone broke. Dropping the dagger, he cried out in pain and backed away.

Eithne, pulled back, a fiery sword extended from her hand and flew toward the gods. Landing near their feet, a wall of fire separated them. Through the flames, *the Dagda* stared at Eithne but soon the fire engulfed where they used to stand and the loud boom that happened earlier to announce them, happened again to signal their departure. When the fire subsided, the field was empty.

Eithne turned to her family, Weylyn still in his full wolf form stood beside her. Her eyes sought out one; Caylean. Without words, he walked forward and with a smile, she touched his chest where his heart beat. "You are much too good to be a mere human. Control your wolf, Hybrid, but be whole once more," she said.

Caylean sucked in a deep breath as her power filled him. Once she released him, he fell to his knees, the little sparks from his fingers showing his powers had returned.

"Use it wisely," Eithne said. Then turning back to her mate, she smiled. But her eyes passed above him to the sky and as the moon rose, she fell to the ground unconscious.

Chapter Fourteen

Aedan stood in awe of his father's mate as she single-handedly defeated the gods. But soon, that awe turned to horror as she fell to the ground, followed by his father's part wail, part howl as he phased back to his human form.

"Eithne!" Weylyn screamed as he pulled her to him. He rocked her back and forth as tears streamed down his cheeks. Aedan felt an echo of his pain. The moon was rising even higher and the sun was setting, Weylyn's mournful wails were all anyone could hear.

Eithne's mother, Selina, the Fae princess, hurried to her daughter's figure and looked helplessly at her husband. Lachlan stood frozen, staring down at his daughter. Alexina took Tristan's hand, Giorsal was helping Caylean up, Labhaoise wiped her eyes as Bowdyn wrapped an arm around her shoulders. Dagda's hand shook until Agora slipped her arm through his and laid her head on his shoulder. Lucien stared down at her, his face contorting in first confusion then sadness as Myrna wrapped her arms around him. Gregor, Nairn and his brother, Diarmad stood back but their woeful gazes were on Eithne and Weylyn.

"Nay," Aedan stated, and Isla went over to him. "She nearly sacrificed her life for mine when I was bitten. She saved my father, both from the wolf's bane and from loneliness. She is my wife's sister and my friend. She lost her mother and father. She lost everything. She is goodness, happiness, hope. I refuse to let her suffer." He looked at Lucien. "I ken there is a way to take a life force and give it to another."

"Aedan," Isla breathed.

He turned to all surrounding them. "You have all been touched one way or another by Eithne. If anyone can look me in the eye and tell me she does nae deserve to live, then I will nae ask anything of you. But if, as I expect, she means much to all of us, then join me and together we will give her life, memories, hope. What say you?"

"Aye," all around him said.

"But how?" Alexina asked.

Kyna squirmed in Isla's arms. Her little form reaching for Lucien, crying. Lucien went to her and took her in his arms.

"What is it, little one?" he asked.

She said nothing, only gave him a power he never felt before.

Save my mother. Please.

"I will," he promised.

Still holding Kyna, Lucien walked over to Eithne and touched her arm. The surge of power turned his eyes red, a color they had not been in years.

Eithne gasped and reared up in Weylyn's arms.

Screaming, the shrill sound echoed across the glen. Then, all went silent.

"Eithne?" Weylyn questioned.

"Weylyn?" she asked.

"Aye," he breathed through his tears. "Aye, love. You remember?"

"Aye, I do," she answered. The vine markings on her arm disappeared. The pointed ears receded back to round, but her red hair stayed fiery unlike the dark auburn it was before.

"You are well?" Weylyn asked.

"Aye, I think so."

"You remember?" he questioned again, desperation in his tone and his face.

"Aye. Weylyn," she tapped his chest then looked around and gasped. "Kyna, my little lass," she reached for her daughter. Kyna squealed and reached for her. Holding her close, Eithne wept. "Thank you."

"Mama," Kyna said.

Eithne sobbed but held her close.

"It is over," Lucien said. "Never again will you succumb to the curse. I felt it leave you."

"As did I," Eithne said. "All thanks to my little one. I love you, Kyna, my warrior lass."

Kyna squealed and snuggled deeper into her mother's chest.

"Eithne?" her mother asked. Eithne looked up to see the Fae standing beside Lachlan, tear tracks on both their faces. Eithne looked to Weylyn and after kissing him, she passed Kyna to him, kissing her forehead.

"Papa," Kyna said. Weylyn grinned through the remaining tears.

"My little lass, I love you," Weylyn said.

Labhaoise helped Eithne stand, as Aedan and Tristan went to help Weylyn up and wrapped one of Aedan's plaid blankets around his waist to shield his nakedness due to his full phase.

Eithne looked toward her parents and took a step closer to them. Selina rushed to her and held her tightly.

"My love," she cried. "I love you so much. Forgive me for the torment you went through."

"I would gladly go through it again so you both could have your soulmate, like I have mine. I am so looking forward to learning more about you both," Eithne said.

"I have watched you grow from afar and I am so proud of you." Selina embraced her daughter. "Little Kyna gave us a chance to be together again too."

"I am so glad we finally were able to meet," Eithne said. "I have so many questions."

"And we will provide answers," Lachlan promised, embracing her. "I have never seen power like that."

"Can I control it?" Eithne asked.

"Aye, I will teach you, my love," Selina stated.

"Thank you… Mama," Eithne finally said. Selina grinned.

"As much as I wish to keep you here with us talking, my sweet one," Lachlan said. "Your soulmate is anxiously waiting the time he can kiss you. Tell him from me, I would be angry if he did not kiss you properly. He has nothing to worry about from me. He has proven in every life he is worthy of you."

Eithne looked back to see Weylyn still holding their daughter, shifting from foot to foot, the plaid draped around his waist, the length falling to his knees making her heart speed. That was a look she knew women would enjoy for many years to come. He looked rugged, handsome and all hers. Squeezing her mother's hand, she headed to him.

Weylyn passed Kyna to Aedan and turned to his soulmate.

"Are you all–" Weylyn did not finish. She fused her mouth to his. "I will take that as an aye," he grinned and pulled her closer to him, kissing her thoroughly to the cheers of everyone around him.

"I love you, Weylyn, Cinioch, Caius, whatever name you go by. I love you."

"Always and forever, my love," he said. "And now, I have eternity to prove it to you."

Another kiss, and Eithne was lost to the sensation of her soulmate's love.

Epilogue

Isle of Skye, Scotland – September 2013

"Kyna? Kyna, love?" she heard her father call.

While her parents, along with Aedan, Isla, Tristan, and Alexina looked at their statue on the Isle of Skye, Kyna studied the architecture of the castle her father, half-brother and alpha helped build. She was certain there was a secret room to the north, just beyond what she remembered was the library. Sitting on the park bench, listening to the songbird tweet its tune, and the humans' conversation, Kyna tucked her dark brown sweater-shrug around her tighter.

It had been over thirteen hundred years since the battle with the gods. Kyna remembered every moment of that day, but nothing else from when she was a baby. As the humans began growing in population, the wolf pack had eventually moved from Loch Alsh to Skye, when Kyna was fifteen and began building the castle before her. She remembered many happy Yules, New Years, Solstices, and yet sad times, too. Not all in their pack were immortal and they mourned those lives lost to time. But as she watched tourists go in and out of the building, she couldn't help but wonder at everything she had seen and all she had yet to experience.

In the years she lived, she had yet to find her soulmate. Though she desired to be loved, she was in no hurry, happy to be independent. She had lovers before. Back in the seventeenth century, they had staying in France for a time and lovers were many to come by and later in the nineteen sixties when *free love* and rock 'n' roll were all the rage, but she had no desire to settle down with a mate, yet.

She scoffed.

Then why, she asked herself. *Am I sitting here waiting on a vision I had, to come true?*

She shared her mother's gift of Second Sight and her most recent vision had been of her meeting someone special on that day.

As she sat, she watched a young couple with a toddler walk past and an ache deep in her core, flared. She had ignored her desire for children, claiming she did not want to pass on the Fae curse to a daughter, but her grandmother and mother both would help teach her daughter, if she had one. Shaking her head, she wondered if the light brown haired, green eyed man she saw in her dream, was her chance for a family and the *always and forever* her parents and packmates drolled on about all the time.

So much for happy to be independent, her wolf spoke up in the back of her mind. She smirked but did not answer the beast. Unlike her brothers, father and even Alpha, her wolf was a separate consciousness and spoke to her often, and she to it. Only Caylean claimed a similar experience with his hybrid wolf, who tamed after the first few years before Kyna was born. But then, he had lost his wolf for a time and the beast, when it came back to him, was much more docile.

"Beautiful, isn't it?" a man said beside her. She looked up, her brown eyes assessing him. He wasn't human, that much she caught from his scent, but he wasn't druid either. Wolf, but only slightly. He looked back at her and her heart skipped. His green eyes were mesmerizing. He was tall, over six feet. His light brown hair glistened almost golden in the sun. He was a Highlander, but even though he was dressed in jeans and a sweater, Kyna could easily see him in a kilt, a fashion her father had started long ago.

"To some," she answered, her accent indicative of where she had lived most of her life; the Scottish Highlands.

"You've seen it before, lass?" he questioned.

"I grew up here," she admitted.

He took a deep breath. "I sensed another immortal but could nae place you. What are you?"

Kyna merely smiled, her light brown eyes curious. The sun parted the clouds and shone down on her reddish-brown hair.

"Why should I tell you?" she asked lightly.

"Fair enough question," he stated. "Alan Conchor," he introduced.

"Kyna Mackinnon," she replied.

"Kyna... may I sit with you?"

"Aye, 'tis a free country, or it will be when we are free of England."

He smiled and sat beside her. "I fought in the battle for Scotland's freedom. *Both* of them, actually. That's when I was turned. A man found me dying on Bannockburn Field."

"My family fought too," she stated. "But is this how you usually start a conversation with a woman? Walk up to her and tell her you're a war hero?"

"No' as often as I would like," he winked.

"Does it work?"

He debated, "no' as often as I would like," he said again, cracking a smile. Kyna giggled and her wolf rolled her eyes. She was like a little schoolgirl.

Independent, my arse, her wolf said. *We are over a millennium old. We have been flirted with before.*

Hush, Kyna told her wolf.

"Interesting," Alan said.

"What?"

"Your eyes flashed to yellow just then," he explained.

"They do that sometimes," she replied.

"I don't mind," he leaned back. "I rather thought it was sexy."

"Bold," she stated.

"No' as bold as asking for your number right after I said that," he winked again.

"Och aye?" she replied. "Are you flirting with me, Alan Conchor?"

"Does it sound like I'm flirting with you, lass?"

"Aye it does."

"Then aye, I am," he teased.

"Kyna, love, where are you?" Weylyn called again.

"Sounds like someone wants you."

"My father," she answered, standing. "And as for my number Alan Conchor, check your phone."

She walked away but stopped and looked back as he pulled out his phone to see a missed call from her. She smiled and blinked. Her name took the place of the unknown number. He looked over at her and grinned.

"There you are, lass," Weylyn said, as Aedan, Tristan, Isla, Alexina, and her mother walked up to her. "We're to meeting your grandparents at lunch."

"The pack will be waiting for us when we return too," Tristan said. "'Tis the Equinox."

"Aye and I look forward to the celebrations," she said. She caught her mother's eye and Eithne's gaze slid to the bench where Alan still sat watching her. She grinned at her daughter and raised her brows. Kyna looked down and breathed a laugh. Her mother would want to know all about the handsome stranger.

"Come then," her father said, oblivious to the exchange and drew her close, kissing her hair.

Her phone chirped. Pulling it out as the rest of the party walked down the drive to the ferry dock, she grinned.

Alan: No goodbye?

Kyna: Was my number not enough?

Alan: Not nearly. I am a half-breed, by the way. My ancestors were named Blane and Odara.

Kyna grinned.

Kyna: I knew them well. Did not realize their descendant would be a half breed.

Alan: Did you? You look good for your age. Somewhere down the line my ancestor married a human. About five generations after Blane and here I am! But the man I met on the battlefield, was a man named Lachlan. He said I would meet my soulmate on the isle, and she would be immortal. Know anyone who fits that description, lass?

Kyna shook her head. Her grandfather was matchmaking again. First with her brother Sèitheach, now her. But Sèitheach was very happy with his mate, maybe Lachlan was on to something.

Kyna: I might. But it took you long enough to get to the isle. What happened? Lost your way? Or did you dogpaddle over?

Alan: Cheeky

Kyna grinned. She was having too much fun and surprisingly her wolf was silent.

Kyna: How about you join us? Local pub. Twenty minutes. I'm sure you can follow my scent.

Alan: Kinky lass, I'd know you anywhere.

Kyna: Prove it.

Kyna felt a sort of giddy feeling as she joined her family on the ferry. Sure enough, her mother caught her alone and peppered her with all kinds of questions about the *handsome man.* Eithne was not only her mother, but her best friend and Kyna made sure to tell her everything, even read the texts to her.

"Well, my love," Eithne said as they stood at the side of the ferry looking out at the icy dark water. "He sounds very interesting. And if your grandfather thought he was good enough for you, then that is a high recommendation."

"Aye," Kyna answered. "He is matchmaking again. I feel sorry for my other siblings. He'll turn his sights onto them soon, if they don't watch out."

Eithne laughed, the melodious sound carrying on the wind. Kyna saw her father turn to look at them when he heard it and smile. No matter where Eithne was, if Weylyn heard her voice or laugh, he looked in her direction. Kyna didn't think he even knew he did it. She could only hope for a mate like him.

Mate now, is it? Her wolf questioned.

Oh hush.

"What is it, love? What does your wolf say?"

"She's reminding me of something I thought of earlier. I was happy in my independence and did not need a man."

"Oh, we women never *need* a man, but it awfully nice

when they're around. And trust me, there is no greater pleasure."

"Mama!" Kyna gasped but laughed along with her.

"It's true and you know it," Eithne replied. "But, sweetheart, just because you might find a male and fall in love, does not mean you cease being independent. Quite the opposite. You are still you and you must always remember that."

Kyna nodded. "I did invite him to the pub. I am curious about him."

"Was he the one from your vision? The one you told me about?"

"I believe he is," Kyna answered.

"Then you fight for him," Eithne stated. "If he is your soulmate, trust me, there is no greater joy."

Eithne looked over Kyna's shoulder toward her husband with such love, Kyna felt a pang of envy. She denied herself even the merest hint of a mate simply because she thought she would never be able to be herself. But now, she didn't want to wait any longer.

"But donnae worry," Eithne went on, her gaze pulled back to her daughter. "I will keep your father distracted. He still thinks of you as his little girl and would not take too kindly to any male coming around you." Kyna giggled knowing full well her father refused to know about any previous lovers she may have had, and still treated her as his little lass. And she wouldn't change him for the world.

Eithne kissed Kyna's cheek and sauntered over to her husband, wrapping her arm around his waist and even slipping her hand down to his arse. Weylyn chuckled but made no attempt to move her hand. Kyna shook her head. Her parents were incorrigible. Gazing out across the water, she decided it was time. Time to stop putting off what she truly wanted. She wanted what her parents had.

One thing was certain, her forever would be more than

just interesting with Alan Conchor in her life. She made a mental note to thank her grandfather when they saw him.

They docked and disembarked. Making their way to the pub, it was crowded with their family and packmates. The September Equinox was a homecoming time for all those who called Tristan *Alpha*. Most were family or related to family down the line. With numerous siblings and cousins throughout the years, their pack counted over three hundred in total. But that day, they met the sixty who had arrived. Kissing cheeks, smiling, and catching up with friends were always some of her favorite things, but that day, her eyes kept drifting to the door of the pub. The *Closed for Private Party* sign hung in the door of one of her brother's great-great-great-grandson's pub, but she hoped, irrationally to see the door swing open and Alan enter.

About two hours later, she had given up when there was no sign of him. Speaking with her cousin thrice removed who had just mated the last moon cycle, she forced a smile when she announced they were expecting and looked at her mate with such love. They were nearly a millennium younger than she was. Taking a deep breath, she excused herself from the group when the conversation turned to another cousin. Heading over to one of the waiting benches by the door, she huffed a sigh and sat down.

Her grandfather; Lachlan sat beside her after ten minutes.

"All right, love?" he asked.

She sighed again. "I'm fine, grampa," she answered.

"No, you're not, tell me what's wrong," he placed his arm around her shoulders.

"Do you believe in true love?" she blurted.

Lachlan leaned away to look at her surprised. He studied her face for a moment, then a soft smile lifted his lips.

"Why do you ask?"

"Do you?" she questioned. His eyes trailed across the

room to her grandmother, standing speaking with her mother and father. Selina usually cast a cloaking spell over her Fae features of green vine markings on her arms and face and pointed ears, to look more human, but when she was with her family, she reverted to her natural look.

"Aye, I do, love," Lachlan replied looking back at her. "I have loved your grandmother for longer than you've been alive. She means everything to me."

"Do you not get... tired of being with the same person?"

"No, because she constantly makes me smile and keeps me guessing. We may be married for over two millenniums, lass, but I see something different about her everyday and I fall in love with her over and over again."

Kyna's eyes turned skeptical. "I assume you're going to tell me she's your *always and forever.*"

"Why do you say it like that?" he asked gently.

"Because not all of us have that."

She huffed a sigh. She may be thirteen hundred years old, but she was acting like a petulant child. But she never realized she wanted what she wanted and the one person she wanted it with didn't want her... her wolf shook her head quickly to try and make sense of what she just thought.

Tell him. Her wolf urged. *He loves us. He would never look down on us or our desires. Papa on the other hand... well, he doesn't want to think about it.*

"What is your wolf saying?" Lachlan asked.

"I met someone," she pronounced.

Lachlan's eyes rose. "Indeed? And when?"

"Just a little bit ago. On the Isle. I donnae ken, 'tis silly."

"Nothing is silly, love. Do you... I hesitate to ask but was it love at first sight?"

"You know I don't believe in that."

"Aye, but was it?"

"I don't know," she admitted. "I thought there was a spark but he's not here."

"You invited him? Is he one of our kind?"

"He is a half breed."

"Ah," Lachlan nodded slowly. "And you invited him here, but he is not here and that has you... upset?"

"No, not upset, merely... perturbed that I allowed myself to feel something again for someone..."

"Love, give him time. If you just met him today... What do you feel?"

Kyna huffed again and then looked at her grandfather. "I felt... what everyone has talked about. I know I have always said I am independent, but I am also lonely. I desire a mate and pups and I feel as if that is not in the gods' plans for me. Maybe it is their way of punishing me still."

"Nay, love. You will have your love. I know it."

"You cannot possibly."

"There is someone out there for everyone, love," he answered. "But I am glad you are focusing on your future and your forever. You have plenty of time."

"Aye, you're right," she answered. Forcing her sadness away, she took a deep breath. "Want to sneak swipes of frosting from the cake?"

"You know how much trouble we get into with your mother every time we do that."

"So?" she teased. "That's what makes it fun."

Lachlan laughed and took his granddaughter's hand. "All right, love. Let's go. We can talk about your always and forever later."

Kyna forced a smile and stood, heading over to the buffet table with her grandfather. Always and forever never meant anything to her… until she saw Alan Conchor saunter into the pub not five minutes later, a grin on his face and a twinkle in his eye. He grinned even more when he saw her, and she realized she had white cake frosting on her nose. Everyone stopped to look at him, someone new and one they did not know. Tristan stepped forward and greeted him. After introductions, Tristan welcomed him to the celebration. He shook hands with those who said hello and embraced those who welcomed him, all while keeping his eyes on her.

Her wolf sat up and took notice of his green eyes and how his smile lit them. He was genuine with everyone he met but he made his way to her still standing frozen by the cake. Icing still on her nose.

"Where have you been?" she asked then kicked herself. She didn't want him to know she was looking for him.

"Sorry, love," he answered. "I missed the ferry. I had to dog paddle."

Och, aye, he would make a fine future.

An Deireadh

Acknowledgements

Goodness, it's finally finished! It is sad and exhilarating at the same time! I cannot say enough *thank yous* to those who have been with me throughout this entire saga! My family, my friends, my readers (many of whom have become friends!), thank you all!

This saga has been a wonderful journey since I returned from a family trip to Scotland and Ireland in 2013! I cannot thank our Scottish tour guide Alan (yes, Alan Conchor was named for him) and our driver Danny! They were indispensable for a young writer gathering all sorts of information. Had Alan not told us the story about how there are no wolves in Scotland, this saga may not have been written, so I owe them a HUGE thank you!

A thank you to my parents who always supports me but also encouraged me to continue working on the story after the first one; *Wolf's Bane*. It was only supposed to be a one book, but the characters kept speaking to me and I had to write their story. Weylyn, Aedan, Tristan, Eithne, Isla and Alexina have been a pleasure to write since the beginning and I love how their lives have unfolded before my very eyes! Their friends and family; Caylean, Giorsal, Dagda, Lachlan, Selina, Gregor, Lucien, Myrna, Labhaoise, and Bowdyn all added a little something to the story.

I am so thankful to have been able to write this story and cannot wait to share it with you! I hope you love this story and characters as much as I have, and I hope you follow me on Facebook, Twitter, and Instagram! Also, keep an eye out for other new releases! If you like shifter novels, I have a dragon shifter story; *Heart of Fire* set to be released at the end of 2019! With a follow up novel *Will of Fire* set for mid-2020!

Thank you for reading and taking the characters into your heart! I hope this last book has given them a wonderful send off! I have to say; I am very happy with how it turned out!

Read on for a sneak peek at: *Heart of Fire*

M. KATHERINE CLARK

Chapter One

Brigid

They say I am a witch. Like my mother, aunts and grandmother. They called us evil, mistresses of Satan, their bane. They say we could talk to animals and we commune with the devil. But what they did nae ken, what they could not know was, witch was nae too far from the truth. Not that I practice black magic or anything like that, or that I would drink goat's blood from a skull, but I am a healer. The ancient practices of my people were well lost to time but there are worse things than to be considered a witch. I keep to myself in the little cottage my mother left me. No one ever told me what had happened to my parents, but I knew. My mother had been burned alive by the heathens who wanted to protect themselves. And my father fell in battle long before. I was but a child when my father kissed me on the forehead and told me to be good before leaving the cottage. I remember seeing my mother crying as she held his tunic in her hands.

Then, she was gone too. Years of healing the clan and then ostracized by the church. I bear them no ill for they believed anything they did nae understand was evil. Maybe I am. But then why do the women of the clan come to me for remedies to prevent them conceiving, or when they need help conceiving? For now, I will stay in my cottage and pretend the world around me was not falling apart.

It is the tenth century and I am in Scotland. I rise with the sun, do my prayers, tend my garden, eat and sleep at moon rise. That is what I have always done in all my twenty years.

As I stirred my porridge for my morning meal, a knock came at my door. I pulled my plaid *aristad* over my head and looked out to see who was knocking at such an hour. Three men I had never seen before, knocked again.

"Mistress," one called. "We are the laird's guards. He has asked to speak with you."

The laird, the bane of my existence and my uncle. "What are your names?" I called out.

"This is Liam and Roger," he said. "And I am Bain."

"Bain?" I questioned.

"Aye, Brigid, 'tis I. We offer nae ill to you," he assured. "We have no weapons on our person apart from our wee knife."

"Send the others away, you know I am nae a threat to you," I called.

It was quiet for a moment until I heard Bain's voice speak again. "I have sent them away. Come out, Brigid."

Bain. He had been my best friend as a lass. One day he was fostered with a neighboring clan and I never saw him again. If this was in fact him, he had grown into a fine man. Opening the door, I gazed into the well-remembered blue eyes.

"Bain?" I breathed.

He smiled and I was taken back to my youth when the world was fair. I stepped forward and offered to embrace him. He wrapped his arms around me, and I took in his familiar smell. Peat, hide, and the musk of sweat, he must have trained earlier today.

"'Tis good to see you, Brig," he said pulling back. "I ken 'tis been a while."

"Years. What are you doing back?"

"Your uncle has called us all to return from our fostering," he replied. "He is troubled."

"By what?" I had not heard anything from the women who came to me for help.

"It would be better if he told you," Bain answered. "Come now, I brought my horse."

"It is not far to walk, I will be fine," I replied. Bain nodded slowly as I turned back to my cottage and doused the kitchen fire. "Lir, stay," I called to my deerhound who lounged beside the hearth. His lazy black eyes looked up at me and he huffed a sigh. Gathering my things, I took some herbs not knowing if I would need any and shut the door behind me.

"You have not changed," he said.

"I have grown," I answered.

"Well, aye into a fine lass, but I meant you are just as stubborn as I recall." He untied his horse from a tree and walked beside me.

"I cannae argue that," I agreed. "But tell me, why does my uncle wish to see me? It is not a usual request."

"As I said, he is troubled," he replied.

"By what?"

"There is a great threat at his door," he answered. "A threat none of us have dealt with before."

"And he believes I will know how to deal with it?"

"I ken no'," he dodged. "All I know is he charged us to bring you to him with all haste."

"And when I get there?" I asked suddenly worried the same fate will befall me as it did my mother, his own sister.

"I donnae ken," he answered.

"Bain," I pressed. "You know what they call me. You know what they did to my mother. Tell me truly, are you leading me to my fate?"

"Brigid, if I knew I would tell you but I was called to bring you to him that is all," he answered.

"Why you?"

"I suppose he knew you may not trust another."

"I have nae reason to trust another, nor you, you have been gone for nearly ten years."

"We are here, Brigid please," he said. "Go to your uncle and see what he wants."

"And will you look me in the eyes as they lower the torch to my pyre?"

"They are not going to burn you," he replied. "'Tis to do with…"

"Ah, so you ken what it is to do with," I cried. "Tell me!"

"Brigid," I heard my uncle's voice boom from the keep steps. Turning to him, I bowed and looked up at his grey eyes. It had been years since I had seen him and the years had not been kind. His young, second wife stood, heavily pregnant, beside him, her eyes downcast. She was no older than me; sold by her family to the great Laird of the isles one year ago.

"Uncle," I said. "You have called for me. How can I help you?"

"I see you are as stubborn as my late sister."

"Donnae dare speak of my mother, it was your hand that lit her pyre!" I spat.

"You will nae raise your voice to me," he bellowed. "You have spent too long on your own you forget I am your laird. Another outburst and you will spend your valuable time in the stocks."

"So says the man who lead my father to battle never to return," I answered. "Tell me what you want from me."

"Guards," he roared. "Seize her."

Screaming, I backed up away from the men who

surrounded me. My eyes locked with Bain, his bitter smirk told me everything.

"Tie her to the stake," my uncle ordered. "For once in her life she may be useful to us."

The men grabbed me but I fought them off.

"Let me go! Donnae touch me! I curse your family and your line for all eternity," perhaps they would stop if they thought I was a witch. But their loyalty to their laird kept them grounded. Far too strong for a small lass like me, the guards soon had me tied to a rough stake, my arms hurt and I was certain I had bruises from their biting grip. I stood there helpless praying for a miracle. I did not want to die. My eyes locked again on my so called friend, Bain's face had changed to an image of my uncle, hard, angry, and bitter. For the first time, I wondered who Bain's father actually was.

"Traitor," I spat. "You were my friend."

"I am nae friend to a witch," he hissed.

"Silence," my uncle bellowed. "Leave her to him."

My eyes snapped to my uncle and grew wide. "To whom?" I demanded. Just as I spoke, a roar like I had never heard before echoed in the bailey.

Chapter Two

Finn

I watched as the humans grabbed the lass, a pretty little thing to be sure but too frail for something like me. But my father had declared it necessary and as his heir I obeyed, my brothers were only too eager to pounce on me. They were too young by half but considered themselves invincible, and granted flying this high and watching the humans with predatory eyes clear as if I were on the ground, gave one a sense of being gods. But I knew better than most that we were not immortal.

When the human guards grabbed the lass, I was impressed by her fighting skills. But soon they over powered her and she was tied to a stake for me. I wondered why she fought so. We dragons were known far and wide for our lovemaking skills and we were fiercely loyal to our mates, forced on us or not. Why did she fight so? Then my stomach dropped when I heard her words. She knew not what was happening to her. She had not been given a choice. I couldn't not help myself I let out a loud roar. This was not what we agreed. I was to be given a willing lass one who agreed to her fate not one who was forced into it.

Her eyes rose sharply to the sky as I circled and landed with a mighty shake. A hush descended on the gathered humans. I was not sure if it was because of my sheer size that they were stunned into silence or if it was because of the lass. But whatever it was, they stared at my glistening green hide. My long neck whipped over to the laird. The old man motioned to the lass, trembling with fear beside me.

"Take her, and may this end to it," he said. An end? I nearly shifted into my human form and charged him with his words. But my father had decreed no human blood was to be spilt. But he did not say I could not scare him a little. Raising one of my talons I covered one nostril and blew fire out of the other, just enough to startled those around me. "Take her and go."

Turning back to the lass, her terrified blue eyes met mine and by all that was holy she was beautiful. Fiery red hair set in a pale freckled face and the bluest of blue eyes stared into my green ones. She was petrified, as gently and softly as I could, I swiped at the ropes holding her, but whipped my tale around the stake so she could not run. When she was free she glanced around her looking for a way to run, but eventually she looked back at me and her eyes grew wide.

Had she never seen a dragon before? Did she not know the legends of the isle? Shaking my head of thoughts, I gently scooped her up in my large talon, barely feeling her striking my scales. She wanted free, but she was mine and I would never let her go back to these humans who treated her as if she were cattle. I beat my massive wings, creating a massive gust of wind. The warriors covered their faces as the dirt beat about them. Finally, I jumped off my hind legs and into the air. The lass screamed as we left the ground and I beat powerfully through the air and into the sky.

Brigid

I am flying. There is a dragon. There is a dragon carrying me and I am flying. I am going to be sick. I am flying. There is a dragon. I kept repeating it over and over again but no matter how many times I said it, it did nae change the fact that there was a large green dragon clasping me in his talons flying away from my clan and the ground. Gripping tightly to the scales, I could not make sense of what was happening. Dragons were a thing of myth, we were living in the second century, there were no such things as dragons, except there was one carrying me high above the ground. Scotland passed by below, all patchwork and dotted with cottages and castles. Where were we going? The sun where was the sun, beside us to my right, south, we were heading south. South from the Islands of my ancestors. But where?

"Ehm, dragon?" I called. The long snout turned down to look at me, the green dragon slits questioning. "Where are we going?" It snorted as if it expected me to be all right with it. "I asked you a question, where are we going?" It said nothing only gripped me tighter. "I demand to know where we are going, who are you?"

Finn

She demands? I chuckled to myself. This tiny human demands to know where we were going? Oh, this will be fun. When I decided to play with my human I was nae sure, but when I felt the pressure in the air drop, I free fell with it. She screeched and clutched tighter.

"You did that on purpose!" she screamed. *Smart little thing,* I thought. Then grinned devilishly to myself. Feeling the air was right, I folded my wings back and spiraled through the patch of wind. Flying backwards, I looked down as I clutched her to my chest. She was grasping to my scales, but was not enjoying herself. Tears rimmed her eyes and it gave me pause. She buried her face into the hard hide of my dragon and wept. I felt the drops not only in my hide but in my heart as well. She did nae ken who I was, what was going on, and she had every right to ask but I played instead of settling her fears. My dragon's protective side roared to life and I held her to me as I searched for a ledge to land. Eventually, I saw the waterfall on the edge of my father's land. It had a large cave behind it. Breaking through the water, I landed gently and shifted into my human form still holding the lass to my chest.